SUBORDINATE CHAOS

By

Kendall Belvedere Helmly

ISBN

Paperback: 978-1-969733-40-6

Hardcover: 978-1-969733-41-3

This is a work of fiction.

Names, characters, places, events, and incidents are either the product of the author's imagination or are used fictitiously. Any resemblance to actual persons—living or dead is coincidental.

Dedication

To Joyce,

and mothers everywhere, the final casualties of war.

Table of Contents

Dedication i

Chapter 1: Ma's Biscuits 1

Chapter 2: Conflicting Letters...8

Chapter 3: Blithering Idiots 16

Chapter 4: Sixty-Four Dollars 21

Chapter 5: Second Thoughts...30

Chapter 6: A Problem in Kansas 36

Chapter 7: Son in Crisis 40

Chapter 8: Justice for Luke 53

Chapter 9: No Accountability 57

Chapter 10: Elizabeth 63

Chapter 11: J. D's Dilemma 74

Chapter 12: A Taste for Blood 81

Chapter 13: Slaughter In the Making 89

Chapter 14: A Storm in Washington D. C..........................96

Chapter 15: Josiah and Daniel Meet 101

Chapter 16: Mae's Trip to D. C...108

Chapter 17: Mackay's On a Mission 114

Chapter 18: Chasing Down a Friend.................................119

Chapter 19: The Trap is Sprung 129

Chapter 20: A Nice Easy Bank Holdup.............................136

Chapter 21: All Aboard for Havana..................................142

Chapter 22: Captured 148

Chapter 23: A Solaced Reunion 155

Chapter 24: A Date With Destiny.....................................159

Chapter 25: Two Coffins 164

Chapter 1:
Ma's Biscuits

My first day as a history professor at Halstead College was going very well so far. I walked up the steps, entered the History Department, and saw my name printed on the door to my office. Dr. Drake T. Crolins. That's me. I walked in, sat down at the desk, and began to organize my personal items around the room when I heard a knock on the door. I said, "Come in, please."

"Hello, Dr. Crolins. My name is George, and I will be attending your class on the Civil War this semester. Part of that curriculum is a thesis, right?"

"Yes, five to six thousand words."

"Professor, sir, I was considering writing about female outlaws/serialists during the war."

"That's a decent topic. Are you familiar with the Anderson Journal?"

"No, sir."

"Start with that. There should be a copy in the college library. If you can't find one, come back and see."

"I will. Thank you, Dr. Crolins." After the enthusiastic young man stepped out, I pulled my personal copy of Dr. Matthew Anderson's war journal off the shelf, sat at my desk, and turned to page one. I read:

May 19, 1866

Ma didn't cotton to preachers. She forced herself into church at Christmas and Easter. The other fifty Sundays Ma was elbow deep in chicken-n-dumplings, one of her specialties. Even her archrival, the Rev. Ames, could not deny how delicious they were, helping himself to at least two helpings every visit. Ma would keep the meals simple on workdays. Breakfast at 7:00 am sharp. Lunch was in the field or in the barn when we had time for a break, consisting of coffee, beans, and biscuits. Supper was at dusk. Day-to-day life on the family farm was the simplest form of chaos anyone could imagine. The days were long, but there was a sweet serenity to most evenings. One could taste the damp coolness of the air as it pushed the sun down past the horizon. I never much enjoyed reading by candlelight, but I always tried to call second dibs on the newspaper after Pa finished reading it.

Local politics kept me entertained. I was always completely engrossed perusing for any fresh war news. Our farm being so close to the Kansas/Missouri border, Pa was always concerned about raiders from the west burning and looting farms that condoned the practice of slave ownership. He feared that sooner or later it would escalate to full-scale war. My folks, Thomas and Willie Mae, raised me, my five brothers, and built a beautiful horse farm together. Both were staunch abolitionists and considered slavery an abomination against God. Love, your brother, your neighbor, and your friend as you would yourself were their answers to forced servitude. They were not pacifists by any means, but slavery was wrong.

Pa was a very personable, charismatic gentleman who liked to pull a cork and pass around the jug from time to time. Despite his abolitionist ideals, he managed to acquire quite a range of social empathy. Most people who met him liked him on the spot. Pa could have been a successful politician if he wanted. Ma probably had a lot to do with his raising horses instead.

Ham, rabbit, and venison with all the trimmings were all staples at the Anderson dining table, provided you were properly washed and your boots were brushed off.

My favorite was Ma's dumplings. We always seemed to have guests for Sunday dinner, invited or not. Mostly, it was neighbors we would run into on the way back from church. Pa wasn't an overly religious man, but he wanted all six of his sons to get their dose of preaching and decide for themselves the consequences of sin. Most Sundays, he would drop us boys off at the churchyard steps, then go pull a cork with his buddies until services ended. Pa was a good provider every day of his life, which ended too soon at the Battle of Farley's Creek; that was 1862. Before that tragic end, our family was well thought of, having the largest horse farm in the county.

Some years we had up to fifty foals per season. Good stock, every single one. Everything from mules to hay burners, we bred them all. It took all eight of us to run the place. Pa was known statewide for being a good judge of horseflesh. We sponsored a horse auction every year on the northeast corner of the farm. The Anderson Farm Horse Auction would bring buyers and spectators numbering in the thousands. Fortunately for us, 1150 acres allowed enough space to accommodate such crowds for the weeklong event. Fortunes were won and lost buying, selling, and gambling on livestock. We routinely entertained Governors, Senators, and even President Buchannan one year. That all came crashing to an end in April of 1861. The Army came and bought almost everything we had. Pa sold all but a dozen horses, six cows, and eight chickens to the Union authorities.

My brothers and I had long since shown our true colors about the impending conflict. Our farm was strictly abolitionist. Ma and Pa refused to condone to practice of slave ownership. The family had agreed if war came, we would sell off the excess livestock and move north to avoid the fighting, but the call to arms was too penetrating for young men like ourselves to ignore. Pa was the first to go and enlist. He was promoted to sergeant. Then Mark and I (Matthew) left for Chicago. My medical degree awarded me a Captain's commission in the Medical Corp. Mark was also commissioned as a Chaplin. Luke and John served as enlisted men in different regiments throughout the war. Ma moved to Springfield and opened a small Restaurant. Again, her dumplings were a favorite among the patrons.

I correspond with her every week, as my brothers did at first. Ma would inform each of us as to the other's situation. I shared much concern over my two enlisted brothers, both serving in combat units. There was much I could tell her in my letters, but I dared not, though I knew full well that she could read between the lines, as I purposely omitted any graphic details.

Many men don't die in combat, but from dysentery, disease, and lack of sanitary living conditions. Despite my intervention at the chain of command, camp life was sometimes deplorable. As the war went on, these hazardous environments were becoming more frequent. Then, of course, there were always the wounded. A sea of red blood saturates the ground in and around every hospital and triage tent. Every battle would bring an endless train of amputations. I ask myself how many yards of enemy territory were paid for by each man's limb? How much for two limbs? How much for the man? My Hippocratic oath obligates me to tend the task at hand. I think this war will not be decided in the same way as others have. Now the politics of battle trumps the sanctity of human life. I fear my capacity for observation of human suffering will be severely tested before this conflict is resolved. It would appear that current weapons technology has morphed the capacity for survival. I observe this subordinate chaos morning, noon, and night. I must shelve my grief, lest I become overwhelmed by this utter madness.

My Brother Mark, the divine prophet, writes:

The displacement of life is only surpassed by the arrogance of command. It cannot be easy for those given the task to force companies of men into battle. I constantly observe the commanders poised like statues in battle from beginning to end. They must accept the outcome and immediately prepare for the next conflict like pieces on a chessboard. Major pieces are exchanged until only the king remains. Gamesmanship is the key to discerning battlefield strategy. Army supreme commanders are the ultimate riverboat gamblers, having to know the precise moment when to call, raise, or fold. When, if ever, does human life slip into the cost analysis?

After the dead and wounded are tallied, the marker comes due. The carts and stretchers pass in review. The day's ugliness is now visible to all. I push down the grotesque lump in my throat, but it drains me. I say a prayer for these fallen many that their sacrifice has not been in vain, that it has significance. A merciful God has a purpose for such unmitigated carnage. What about the conflict itself? Both armies cannot achieve their ultimate goal. Conflicting ideologies have brought them to this armed struggle over hallowed ground. God spare us this tumult in human agony. I must retire now and find inspiration for the new dawn. Matthew, my brother, my wishes for a swift end to this conflict have fallen by the wayside. On that, we can certainly both agree. I wish you good fortune.

God's speed and safe return, Mark

I write Ma, deleting any notion of despair; there is no value in dwelling upon human indignities. Instead, I will mention the things I miss. The smell of biscuits is hot and fresh from the oven. Fighting with my brothers for the last bit of preserves in the jar. Watching her laugh while putting another jar on the table, or seeing the reverend Ames' shirttail ravel out of his pants after stuffing himself with dumplings.

Dear Ma,

How are things at the restaurant? I hope you are busy in these very unpredictable times. I am continuing to tend the wounded in my regiment. Doctors, nurses, and corpsmen are in short supply throughout the Army. Unfortunately, I am very busy working my trade. I surely do miss your cooking. I miss you and the brothers dearly. I got a letter from Mark recently. He seems to be settling into his position as Chaplin. I sincerely look forward to a swift and immediate end to this conflict, but I fear that it may go on for a while. After the war, I would like to open a private practice somewhere in St. Louis or Springfield. It's getting late, and my candle is getting short. All my love.

Matthew

Ma's Christian name was Willie Mae Sims. She came into the world kicking and screaming, a good sign of being a healthy baby. She was the third child and second daughter born to Art (short for Arthur) and Sara Sims on January 9, 1819. A cold, blustery day. Mae's folks ran a Trading Post just outside Fort Ticonderoga in upstate New York. Before long, she showed a very strong aptitude for arithmetic and began clerking for the customers. She sure had her mother's looks and kept a steady stream of suitors coming in to trade, which didn't do Art's heart any good. The way she constantly flirted with all the young boys who came by used to rile Arthur quite a bit sometimes. Mae always knew when she crossed the line. Art would scoff and send her off to balance the daily ledger. Some Saturdays, Mae would end up syphering the ledger over a dozen times. It was his way of saying he loved her. Two months after Mae's seventeenth birthday, a tall, dark hunk of a young man walked through the door, and no amount of syphering was going to keep them apart. Thomas Daniel was the youngest son in the Anderson family, who had a small spread further south on the Hudson River.

Tommy and Mae were married in a simple ceremony and headed west to seek their fortunes. They got as far as St. Louis. Eight months later, I was born (oops, shotgun wedding). No bother, they had enough love between them for ten newlyweds. Thomas and Mae prospered as fur traders. A skill Thomas inherited from his father while trapping and hunting along the banks of the Hudson River. Soon, they scrimped and saved enough to purchase a small farm south of Springfield, and the baby boys kept coming. All of Mae's midwives would tease her unmercifully; it was Tom's fault they didn't have a girl yet. They told her that Tom had to stick it in nine inches for a girl to pop out, but alas, six boys in a row. Soon, leather hides and pelts would transition to horses and other livestock. This would prove highly profitable prior to the war between the states. Settlers heading west needed livestock to get where they were going. A good team of horses would get a wagon to Fort Hays, but for a trek to Oregon, one needed oxen. Slow and steady will get you to the West Coast. Tom and Mae contemplated selling out, packing up, and heading for California during the gold rush in 1949, but the money was too good selling livestock in Missouri. Had they known more about the shitstorm brewing in Washington over slavery, they might have thought better of relocating to Northern California.

Chapter 2:
Conflicting Letters

There would be no turning back after shots had been fired on Fort Sumter on April 12, 1861. War in all its chaos, fury, honor, nobility, savagery, and madness would now unfold upon the American people. The president was now faced with the threat of armed combat. Mr. Lincoln and the Southern States, calling themselves the Confederate States of America, were at an impasse. No amount of diplomacy, negotiation, or compromise would belay the irreconcilable differences separating the two polarized ideologies. Once the South Carolina State Militia fired upon the Union garrison in Fort Sumter, a hateful conflict was now set in motion. The war would continue for almost four years. Battles were long and bloody. It would last until April 9, 1865. Just a mere six days prior to Mr. Lincoln's death at the hand of an assassin's bullet.

Lincoln was a relatively young man when he took the oath of office on March 4, 1861. The constant setbacks thrust upon the Army of the Potomac gave him very little to be optimistic about. He could not find a Supreme Commander who could compete with General Lee on the battlefield.

Tom Anderson and his abolitionist friends campaigned hard to make Missouri a free state. Unfortunately, the Missouri Compromise rebutted their efforts until the war was over. Slavery is the annexation of human dignity for mammon. Individuals who work and profit from the sale of human flesh lie upon the devil's apron for a good night's sleep. Many of the founding fathers sought to end an injustice that should never have been allowed to exist after 1787. Our founding fathers became the great appeasers by giving in to North Carolina, South Carolina, and Georgia.

Thomas and many of his neighbors were united in the fight to eradicate slavery in Missouri. His Quaker upbringing had predisposed him to see all men made in God's image as equal. He would lie awake at night staring up at the stars, imagining heaven as a place where there were no limits to the goodness of the human spirit. Tom's father told him on several occasions that the color of a man's skin matters not in the eyes of God. We are all put here on this earth to help one another; the greatest sin that anyone can commit in this world is to ignore the suffering of others. Love thy neighbor as thyself (Mark 12:31). Father was an eloquent man, full of grace and compassion. Seeing the world as a market for equilateral prosperity was reason enough to find empathy for those in bondage. Those words would spark a deep desire to speak out for the abolishment of slavery in any form. It was unfortunate that Tom would not live to see the ratification of the Thirteenth Amendment.

Tom had never had the opportunity to socialize with any person of color until he became a soldier. James Bernard Smith, aka Jimbo, was a runaway slave who was tasked as a grave digger in Tom's unit. The 3rd Missouri Union Volunteers took part in multiple engagements from late 1861 to early 1865. Lots of mud, blood, and marching, miles and miles of marching. Some days his unit would cover over forty miles between bivouacs or camps. Jimbo's tent was near Tom's. When the opportunity would present itself, they would converse. Simple topics at first, but later, social conflicts and politics were discussed. It turned out that Jimbo was a carpenter's apprentice on the Smith plantation in the northeast corner of Missouri. The second son of James Alias, the lead carpenter on the Smith plantation.

That was until Tennessee rebel forces looted, burned, and killed almost every living soul on the plantation in early 1861. Jimbo and the other surviving freed Negroes were sold back into slavery. During the exodus to Georgia, with their new owner, Jimbo and the others managed to overtake their captors and confiscate all the supplies. After the escape, they agreed to split up and flee separately, hoping to increase their odds of securing freedom again. Two days on the run, Jimbo ran into the 3rd Missouri. Jimbo was fortunate; most of his family did not fare as well as he did. Unknown to him, his siblings were caught just days after escaping.

Life as a slave in South Georgia was harsh. His two brothers were made to work in the cotton fields. Jimbo's sisters were subsequently sold to neighboring farms. They would be subjected to sexual abuse almost daily. Ruthless, rich southern slave owners made the most of opportunities to breed their slaves due to the inability to export more from Africa after the Act Prohibiting the Importation of Slaves became law.

Tom was relieved that the men in his squad did not chastise him for befriending Jimbo. Most of them were indifferent simply for lack of exposure to Africans.

Most residents of the Midwest states and further north had never encountered a black person. Slavery was an indignity left mostly to the Deep South. Time was, many living far north considered it a travesty, but it didn't exist in their community, so they didn't concern themselves with customs and controversies hundreds of miles away. It had no bearing on New Jersey or New Hampshire, so why expend the effort getting involved? That all changed with the passage of the Fugitive Slave Act.

Referred to by many abolitionists as the Bloodhound Bill, it would present a huge hurdle to the eradication of slavery in the U. S. Individuals aiding runaway slaves were subject to federal prosecution.

Ma had similar feelings toward abolition, and she hated the war. This did not sit well with some of her neighbors.

"To hell with the neighbors. This war is wrong. Your father, Matthew, and Mark will be killed, sure as anything. I tell you now, John, this war is not going to be settled quickly. It will go on for years and solve nothing. Our livestock is gone, and land prices are down. 1150 acres, we would be lucky to get two dollars an acre for the land, and five hundred dollars for the buildings."

"Ma, you don't really want to sell the farm, do you?"

"Yes, your dad gave the right to sell the place to your older brother, Luke. I am seriously considering selling out and heading for California. I could open a restaurant, a dress shop, or both. Come with me and your younger brothers."

"Ma, Luke, and I both want to enlist in the Union Army."

"I know. I heard you talking up in your room months ago. So, you both have made up your mind to do this. You do know if all five of you get killed? I will be left to raise your younger brothers by myself. Tommy Jr. is a handful, and Andrew ain't much better."

"Yes, regrettably, that could happen, but I don't think this war will go on more than a year. I think by then the war will be too expensive for both sides to continue. It costs a large amount of money to feed and supply all those men. One or both sides will sue for peace."

"When did you take such an interest in politics?"

"Since I started working down at the General Store. That's all anybody can talk about these days. I heard Mayor Preen say to Marshall Hendricks that the Confederate Army is a bunch of ragtag misfits who could not whip a jackrabbit."

"I got news for you, kid. Some of those soldiers are tough as barbed wire and twice as mean. You decide to go on and enlist, then you better be willing to fight for your life in every single battle. I promise you that some big Johnny Reb is going to rip you in half just the same as looking at you. You better be ready to shoot, stab, punch, kick, slap, whatever it takes to stay alive. Are you prepared to sell yourself for an idiom? That is how you survive a war, by staying resolute to finding a means to the end. Kill until no enemy is left. Can you do that?"

"No matter, Ma, I have to join this fight." Ma could have talked for another week, and it wouldn't have changed Luke or John's minds. Ma knew it was hopeless to continue trying to hold onto the farm. She and the four remaining boys went into town the following Monday and sold the entire estate. Half a life's work consolidated into a check for $2,800. Ma gave Luke and John two hundred dollars each and said goodbye. They headed for St. Louis to enlist in the Union Army. Ma, Andrew, and Tommy packed up their grips, tossed them into a covered wagon, and headed for California. Their first stop was Fort Hays in Kansas. They joined a wagon train headed for Oregon, with continued passage to San Francisco, California. The trip would take almost five months to arrive in California. Immediately after arriving in San Francisco and securing adequate housing, Ma started writing to all her soldier boys back east. It took nine months before the first letter came, but it was not what she expected. The letter was from Thomas' commanding officer describing the surroundings of his death during The Battle of Farley's Creek. Colonel Welch sounded very sincere in describing how my father died in battle. The man spoke of Thomas's bravery and courage, exalting dad with multiple praises, raving on about how father died a heroic soldier's death. Ma was less distraught by the letter than I expected. I surmised that she had long prepared herself for this situation. Three weeks later, another letter came from Private Lance Hudson, a soldier who fought alongside Thomas. He told a quite different tale leading to Pa's death.

Dear Mrs. Anderson,

My name is Lance Hudson. If you are not already aware, your husband, Thomas, has been killed. I am very sorry for your loss. Thomas was my squad leader and a good friend to everyone in our unit. I understand that you and he raised six sons on your horse farm in Missouri. When he described it, I was reminded of my own family farm in Ohio. The main reason I am writing to you is to let you know I would not be alive right now if it weren't for your husband. Our squad was ordered to advance on the enemy during The Battle of Farley's Creek. There was so much confusion that morning. As we started to march forward, a cannonball headed straight for me and severed my left leg clean off just above the knee. I fell to the ground and just lay there in such pain. Thomas grabbed my belt and secured it as a tourniquet so that I would not bleed to death. Then he carried me back to the tree line a couple of hundred yards away. I would eventually be escorted back to the rear by a pair of orderlies. The surgeon who operated on me said I was very lucky. He told me most men bleed out in minutes. My fighting days in this war stopped almost as soon as they started. I consider myself lucky to have only lost half a leg.

A few days later, when I started to recover and gain all my faculties again, I asked where your husband was. I wanted to thank him for saving me that day. I was told by a buddy of mine Sgt. Anderson was killed during a bayonet charge later that day. Apparently, he fought valiantly despite us losing the battle. I don't remember much up to the point of my leg being blown off by that screaming cannonball. I will never forget that sound. It seemed like I had heard it coming forever. As for the battle, the officers in charge seemed confused about everything. We drilled and prepared for months in preparation for battle. Then, when it finally came, nobody really knew what was going on. I saw hundreds of dead men being carted off from the hospital where they stitched up what was left of my leg. Our division commander, General Crawford, was also killed during that battle. I heard the general was shot off his horse, waving his Sabre in the air. The entire day was complete bedlam. No one seemed to know what anyone else was doing. If this is a sampling of what the battles are going to be like, we are in for a very long and bloody conflict. I don't mean to make light of my injury, and certainly of your husband's death. I guess I just wanted you to know the circumstances surrounding his demise.

A few days after I was released from the hospital, I was put on light duty. I was transferred to Regimental Headquarters as an enlisted staffer. Mostly, I just hung around the officers' quarters and ran errands. Between errands, I would hear the Captains and Lieutenants talk about how bad the campaign was going. They would talk of how chaotic it was. Several of them admitted to pissing on themselves during battle. Who knows, I might have done the same thing or worse if I hadn't lost my leg so quickly. It has become very apparent to me that whatever orders the Commanders are giving their junior officers are not being carried out. Entire companies of men were being slaughtered during every battle. I probably shouldn't be telling you this, but I don't think our field commanders are up to the task of winning this war. If you could write to me and let me know that this letter found its way to you, I would be grateful. I am now serving the rest of my enlistment in a telegraph office in St. Louis. I am and will always be eternally grateful to your dear husband for saving me from a most horrifying death. God bless you and your family always.

Sincerely,

Private Lance Hudson

Ma was not at all happy upon reading the second letter. Honestly, she was genuinely pissed off about the whole thing. The letter stayed in her apron pocket for weeks. I told Ma to burn the letter. She refused, citing that God put this letter in her hand for a reason, and until it becomes clear why, she was going to keep it by her side.

Chapter 3:
Blithering Idiots

Ma wasted no time in answering Private Hudson's letter. She thanked him for being so candid about the circumstances of Father's death. Ma wrote to me about how Private Hudson described the complete lack of ability shown by Dad's Field Commanders. I could tell by the unabridged wording that she was angry, spouting accusations of incompetence and belligerent stupidity on the part of those so-called men of stature in charge.

As a physician, I am put in a very awkward position. So, few men pass through my hospital able to return to their units at full combat readiness. Most of the injuries sustained by soldiers leave them dead or incapacitated to the point of just being able to carry on, much less combat effective. I ask myself, am I contributing to soldiers' deaths by making them healthy enough to fight again? I can't let myself look at it that way, or I will agonize over every soldier I treat with a bad case of poison ivy. That certainly will not keep them out of the war.

I can sympathize with Ma. She definitely has a point about many of the Union Field and Staff officers not having the grit or gumption to lead men in combat. I see wounded officers cry like babies next to enlisted men with more serious wounds who remain reticent, waiting for me to patch them up. That is not completely fair; it can depend on the nature of the wound. Though I have seen many lieutenants sob over a dislocated shoulder or a broken finger. Still, it is the duty of every soldier to face the enemy when called upon to do so, regardless of the circumstances. All the subordinates can hope for is a favorable outcome, allowing them the opportunity to walk away from the days of fighting and live to skirmish another day.

So, who is to blame for the damning outcome of war? Is it the politicians who declare it? What about the Generals who are forced to play God with soldiers' lives, passing down orders to Regimental Commanders, deciding what unit attacks first, and what unit waits in reserve? Is it the private soldier who rushes forward during a bayonet charge and faces an enemy soldier, then runs him through, lest they be stabbed and suffer the same fate? There are no innocent men at the end of a battle, only casualties to be counted and blood-stained ground gathered as spoils. Battle for battle, life for life, acre for acre, and grave for grave, who shall we call out to answer for the multitudes of fallen brave?

Ma sees no justice in this conflict. I fear she will mourn deeply at the loss of her loving husband for quite some time. I have not heard from Luke or John for months. The last I heard, Luke was in a Cavalry unit headed for Kentucky. He was always the best horseman on the farm. John wrote me that he was in an Artillery unit headed for Kentucky, also, although that was over four months ago. I guess I can take some solace in the fact that neither brother is in an infantry unit. Dad sure didn't last long in his first major battle.

It's quiet now, in the cool of the evening. I reminisce back to the family farm, recalling similar evenings. After the horses were put to bed, just prior to dusk, the brothers and I would gather on the front porch with Dad and share a quiet moment watching the last flicker of daylight pass under the cover of nightfall. Seven young men gathered, sharing one ideology, securing the family legacy. My brothers and I were a bit younger then. At seventeen, I was the oldest and chomping at the bit to head off to Philadelphia for Medical School. I never envisioned a scenario where I would end up an Army surgeon. War punishes men way beyond any medical capability. Every officer call, that's my cue to prepare myself for the stampede of wounded suffering through agonizing trauma. I save as many as I can, as fast as I can. That is all my skills as a doctor will allow. I know my place in the grand politics of war. My personal idioms of peace in this conflict will have to remain silent until the last order is given to fire at will. I returned to my tent to find a letter from Ma on my pillow.

Dear Matthew,

I hope this letter finds you well. Your brothers and I are settling into life in San Francisco. It is quite the boomtown. Gold dust is everywhere. I decided to open a mercantile/trading post in lieu of a dress shop. The boys and I can barely keep up with all the googly-eyed tinhorn prospectors still flocking to California. The biggest issue so far has been transferring merchandise from the wholesaler to our store. I hired the services of a former lawman/gunfighter who goes by the name, Irish J. D. Malone. Since hiring him and his outfit, I haven't lost a shipment. You would like him. He isn't as grounded as your father was, but similar to Thomas in many ways. Mostly, he is honest. He does tend to get liquored up now and then, but not on the job.

I see in the papers that the war is not going very well. It seems that Mr. Lincoln is having trouble finding a commander who doesn't have his head up his ass all the time. Don't get me started on that subject. I still feel very strongly that the men in charge are not qualified to complete their assignments. I mean, I know that it can't be easy for them to order men to engage the enemy. I just think they could be going about it a better way. Hey, what do I know? I only raised six boys and fed the eight of us three times a day every day we lived on our farm. What kind of organizational skills could I possibly have??

Andrew and Tommy were chomping at the bit to join the Union until I threatened to send J. D. Malone after them. I told you I like that gunslinger, maybe too much. It's late here, and I have a big day tomorrow. the weekends are always crazy around here.

I wish you well,

Love, Ma

It sounds like Ma has a boyfriend. I am glad that someone is mentoring my little brothers while I am not around to beat some sense into them. The last thing this war needs right now is another pair of Billy badasses who think they can defeat the entire Confederacy by themselves. Ma seems to be doing well financially. I am glad to hear that, and I am ecstatic that War is over a thousand miles away from them right now. I do hope that it stays that way. I miss Ma and all my brothers. If my unit stays bivouacked, I will write everyone a letter tomorrow, but I suspect the unit will get marching orders, based on the last officer's call.

Dusk has taken center stage; the only thing stirring around camp right now is the posted centuries and junior officers still on duty. Every hour of the day has a small contingent of soldiers on guard to secure the perimeter and fire watch in camp. There are pickets scouting the area for any enemy advancement as well. There is not much chance of us being raided tonight. We are miles behind the front lines. The scuttlebutt going around is that the unit will be called up in reserve for an upcoming attack in the morning. Everything will start over again at 0500. That's 5 am for me; I still haven't bought into military time yet. Breakfast will consist of a salt pork strip and hard tack. My shift in the infirmary doesn't start for another hour.

Corporal Reins came running toward me, "Captain Anderson, you are needed in the infirmary right away."

"Thank you, corporal."

"Yes, sir." I immediately checked in. Lieutenant Roberts informed me of four new cases of dysentery within the past half hour.

"Lieutenant, wake up the mess sergeant and get his ass over here double quick. Let's see if we can't figure out what the culprit is this time."

About ten minutes later Sgt. Bickell walked into the tent and reported it to me.

"Sgt, are you cleaning the serving utensils prior to serving chow like I ordered you to? We just received four new cases of dysentery after chow tonight. I expect there will be more in the morning. Well, Sgt!!"

"Sir, ever since the last episode, I have been boiling the utensils prior to serving every meal. Begging the Captain's pardon, but I don't believe this was a case of dirty spoons. Sir, we haven't had a case of dysentery for over ten days since I started boiling the spoons before serving."

"Very well, then check your meat rations for fecal matter."

"Fecal matter, sir?"

"Yes, rat and or mouse turds, check them right away. Move out!"

"Lieutenant, if he finds half a mouse turd in the salted pork barrels, I will see to it personally that he digs every latrine for the duration of the war. The meat coming out of those barrels is not much in the way of edible anyway, we are going to have to increase the frequency of health inspections in the Mess."

"Yes, sir, Captain."

"James, I will officially relieve you now. Go ahead and get some sleep. We are in for a long day tomorrow."

"Thank you, Captain."

Chapter 4:
Sixty-Four Dollars

The rain just kept pouring down off and on all morning. Andrew and Tommy Jr. minded the store while Ma went over to the bank to make the weekly deposit. Two drovers walked in the front door and grabbed a handful of cigars, three plugs of tobacco, ten pounds of bacon, six cans of beans, two skinning knives, and a case of .45 ammo.

Andrew announced, "That will be sixty-four dollars even for your purchase."

The larger of the two men opened up his duster to reveal two revolvers. he placed his right hand on one of the handles and said, "Paid in full, right?"

"Yes, sir. Paid in full." The two men walked out, mounted up, and proceeded a hundred yards down the street and entered the "Painted Pony Saloon." The boys went back to stocking shelves, trying to forget the entire incident. Ma walked in and asked if anyone had come in while she was at the bank. Andrew and Tommy just looked at each other and immediately hung their heads.

"Okay, boys, what happened?"

Andrew spoke up, "A couple of drovers came in and took sixty-four dollars in merchandise without paying. The big fella flashed his pistols at us, grabbed the stuff, and rode down to the 'Painted Pony' with his partner." Ma grabbed her pistol belt, fastened it around her waist, grabbed the sawed-off twelve-gauge shotgun and a handful of shells from under the counter, and headed for the door.

"Come on, boys, it's high time you two learned how to take care of business." Ma locked the front door and hung the "Be back in 15 minutes" sign. Then the three of them marched down the street to settle the bill. Ma stopped in the doorway of the saloon and told Andrew to point out the two men.

"There they are, Ma, bellied up to the bar. The two wearing the deer shin dusters."

"Okay, boys, walk behind me and stay close to the door." Ma walked past the doorway slowly, hiding the sawed-off shotgun behind her, on the way to the bar. She bellied up right next to the larger of the two men and ordered a whiskey.

The big man spoke up, "Barkeep, it's on me. My pleasure Mam!"

"Begging your pardon, sir, but you don't get to buy me my drink."

Puzzled, he asked, "Why is that?" Ma whipped the loaded and cocked shotgun around and shoved it right up in the man's neck and shouted, "Not until you pay the bill you owe me at my store! Sixty-four dollars, let's see it right now!"

"Ok, ok, it's in my shirt pocket!"

"Get your hands up and keep um' up!" Then Ma drew her pistol and pointed it at his partner. "You, peckerwood, get your hands up too. Andrew, get over here, now! Take sixty-four dollars out of his pocket."

"Yes, Ma, right away!" Andrew retrieved the money and returned the remainder to the man's pocket.

"Okay, sir, our business is done. Do you still want to pay for my drink?

"I respectfully decline." Then Ma announced to the entire bar, "Now my boys and I are going to go now. Everybody is just going to relax and have another drink. Good day to you, gentlemen."

The big man quipped to his partner, "That woman is going to regret that." The bartender spoke up, "No, she won't. That's J. D. Malone's girl. You are lucky he wasn't here, or you both would be picking your teeth up off the floor." The two drovers finished their drinks quietly and exited the bar without incident. That was the last time either of those bums was seen in the Frisco area.

The three of them marched right back to the store. "Well, boys, what did I tell you about looters and thieves. Always keep your wits about you and stay near the sawed-off shotgun when trash like that walks in. Don't flinch, keep your edge. That's how you have to deal with a threat. You boys quit on yourselves. Come on, there's a nice venison stew on the stove, dealing with those bums gave me an appetite. Besides, J. D. will be arriving on the evening ferry with more supplies, and I want to eat something before he gets home. Tommy, go to the post office and see if we have any mail. We will eat it when you get back."

Tommy returned about twenty minutes later with a letter addressed to Mrs. Willie Mae Anderson. the return address was an APO (Army Post Office) in Kentucky from a Colonel Tuberville. Ma studied the letter for some time before opening it. Andrew and Tommy suspected that it was a death notice for Luke or John. Sure enough, John died after suffering a bullet wound to the chest. The surgeons removed the bullet, but he lost too much blood and died a day later. Needless to say, Ma and the boys all lost their appetites. It started to rain again. Ma sat in the rocker on the storefront porch for what seemed like an eternity. Then she promptly arose out of her chair and went upstairs, took a bath, and went to bed.

About an hour after dark J. D. Malone and his crew arrived from Oakland. They unloaded the wagons and ate all the venison stew before retiring to the bunkhouse for the night. J. D. headed up to Ma's room. He knocked on the door. Ma opened the door and asked J. D. to join him. They talked for quite a while during J. D's bath in the porcelain claw-foot bathtub. This would be the first of many nights that the two of them would share a bed together.

"So, you shook down a couple of bums today. I would have given anything to have seen that. Andrew said he and everybody else were petrified the whole time, especially the guy with the shotgun in his face. I knew you were a very formidable woman, but to pull that off takes real nerve. Would you really have blown the guy away for a lousy $64?"

"He threatened my boys over that lousy $64, so yeah, I would have shot both of them. I had to eliminate the threat, just the way the animals do. There's only room in the pasture for one bull; all the others run off or get killed."

"Mae, you are a hard woman."

"I have to be in order to survive in this community dominated by men. I can't afford to back down, not even once."

"I was sorry to hear about John. Tommy informed me you got the letter today from his commanding officer."

"I did; I don't really want to discuss it right now. I just want you to hold me really tight and kiss me again and again. Can you do that for me?"

"You know I can, sweetheart." The next day, it was all over town how Mae faced down two gunmen who tried to rob her. The story even made the papers. They called her "Scattergun Mae Anderson." She was quite the celebrity for several weeks. It did bring lots of new business to the store. Everyone wanted to buy their panning and mining gear from her.

The notoriety started to fade just about the same time she got a letter from Corporal Sam Talbin. Much like with Pa, she received a letter describing in much more detail the circumstances surrounding John's death. Not the least of which was the fact that he was killed because his commanding general failed to recognize the enemy right in front of him.

Mrs. Anderson,

My name is Sam Talbin, and I was a Corporal in your son John's unit prior to his death. This may come as a grave shock to you, but John was killed by a soldier donning the blue, not the gray. I lost the use of my left leg due to artillery fragments during the same engagement. I write to you out of the deepest respect I have for John. I never met a more decent and upstanding individual in my life. In between battles, camp life can get really boring. All we did was drill every day. That got old real quick. Your son and I would sneak off to a nearby creek or pond and catch our supper. John always managed to hook something. He caught a huge catfish one afternoon. We ate real good that night.

You are probably wondering about the circumstances of his being mortally wounded. Nothing would please me more than to tell you he died valiantly, saving other men's lives on the battlefield. The ugly truth is we both sustained injuries due to a blundering field commander. Our less-than-competent leader, General Miller, failed to scout the battlefield just prior to ordering our advancement. It turned out that the unit that he thought was one of ours was actually a rebel militia who were issued blue coats instead of gray. They wiped us out. Half of our unit was dead before the general called for retreat. Surprisingly, General Miller was left in command after the battle. Lucky for me, my days of soldiering are over. I mustered out a little over a week ago. Now I am only half the man I was prior to the start of this useless war.

John mentioned that you and his two youngest brothers pulled up stakes and moved to California. I would really like to come and visit you and your family one day. John also said you opened a general store in San Francisco. I don't suppose you could use a broken-down ex-soldier like me. I don't want to seem forward, but as I have no real prospects right now, I could really use a job in the worst way right now. I do tend to hobble around quite a bit, but it can't be helped.

Sometimes I wish that I was back on my old family farm before it was destroyed by the Missouri Raiders. They killed my Ma and younger sister while Pa and I were away on business, attending a livestock auction in Hays, Kansas. I forgot to mention I grew up about fifty miles outside of Hays. My Ma and Pa were sooners from way back. It was a beautiful spread. We mostly raised hogs and goats for a living. One nice thing was that we always had meat on the table. Ma was a great cook. That all changed in a heartbeat, a little over a year ago. After the raid on our farm, Pa took to drinking. He couldn't handle the loss of Ma and my sister Amy. For a short while, I was right there with him at the saloon every night, until I got in a fistfight with the Sheriff's nephew. The next day, I went to Fort Hays and enlisted. There is probably a wanted poster for me in Kansas right now. The kid kept spouting on about Southern states' rights. So I broke his nose with my fist and kicked him in the ribs a few times before Pa grabbed me and threw me out of that saloon.

I know I shouldn't be burdening you with all my dirty laundry, but after talking with John and listening to him dote upon you so much, I feel like you are someone who may understand how I felt right then. I was angry, really angry. not just at the rebels for destroying my family, but I was mad at God for letting it happen.

Right now, I am just disappointed that everything changed so quickly. I find myself having to wash out spittoons for a living. I quit drinking. I know now if I crawl back inside a bottle, I will never get back out again.

I hope this letter gives you some closure as you grieve the loss of your boy. I do hope to meet you sooner or later, someday.

Sincerely,

Sam Talbin

Ma finally stopped crying long enough to read the letter to Andrew, Tommy, and J. D. It was a very somber moment. Ma poured herself a shot of whiskey and gulped it down, then another. J. D. grabbed the bottle off the table and said, "That's no way to grieve, didn't you learn anything from the letter you just read us?"

"Yes, I surely did. I want to see General Miller's bloody corpse at my feet. How the hell does a general not know the enemy in front of him? Tell me that Major Malone, hero of the Mexican-American War!"

"Ok! War is chaos. Friendly fire and failure to recognize the enemy kill a lot of soldiers. This war is different from others in that respect. It has Americans fighting Americans. Artillery units aren't always given the right locations to shoot. It's not an exact science. If the enemy isn't where the commander expects them to be, it gets complicated. A retreat could send the bulk of his army right into a rebel ambush."

"Didn't they teach you anything at the academy?"

"Yes, they did, but most of the tactical stuff is based entirely on lessons learned from previously fought battles."

"So, you end up making the same mistakes they did!"

"No, Mae, hopefully we learn not to make the same mistakes."

"Fat chance of that!"

"Look, sweetheart, I know you feel extremely passionate about this right now, but this is not a healthy way to grieve the loss of John. Revenge is never a good answer. The cemeteries are full of prideful men hell bent on avenging the death of a relative. It never ends well for anybody. Remember what was best in John, what brought him joy. That's how we should mourn his passing."

"Well, the best thing about John, and the boys will back me up on this, was his kind nature. He loved the animals we raised. The horses would gather around him in the corral. It was as if he were really having a conversation with them. I still don't get why he didn't end up married. For such a handsome man to stay single as long as he did was quite a trick. Becky Saunders practically threw herself at him at the last Fourth of July picnic we had. It was a bit shameless. Her hormones were raging that day. God help her future husband on their wedding night. There must have been half a dozen girls interested in John around that time. That was July of 1860. Lots of changes in the last two years. With Matthew and Mark being career soldiers, I don't see any prospects for grandchildren any time soon. I am glad they both chose a profession as far away from combat as possible. Even as POW's they receive fair treatment. Thank you, J. D. I am feeling much better now. I'm still mad as hell, but you are correct, putting someone's head on a pike won't make things better for anyone." J. D. put his arm around her as they snuggled together on the settee.

J. D. abruptly changed the subject, "Tomorrow is Sunday, the three of you are going to get a shooting lesson from me. I don't want to have another incident like you boys had several weeks ago ever again. One thing I learned very early on as a lawman is, there are two kinds of people who carry a gun. Those who will show it to you in their holster, and men who will actually point it at you. When someone points a loaded pistol at you, that is the time to worry. In your case, as soon as that drover opened his duster, I would have grabbed the shotgun and pointed it at his chest. Trust me, nobody likes looking down the barrel of a shotgun. That will convey your intentions immediately. It is not easy to alleviate a threat like that. You must have the courage to stand your ground.

Courage is pushing fear aside to stay alive. The willingness to fight or not to fight depends on the threat."

Tommy interjected, "How do you know when to fight?"

"That comes from experience, or by listening to others who have faced death. For the two of you, that would be your ma and I. Pay heed to what we have to say. It may save your life one day."

Chapter 5:
Second Thoughts

J. D. was starting to be a little apprehensive about taking his relationship with Mae to the next level. She is loving and supportive of J. D. and her family, but definitely shows a vindictive side at times. Mae stood at the base of the stairs and said, "Good night, boys. J. D., are you coming to bed?"

"Right behind you, sweetheart," Mae walked upstairs and entered the master bedroom, undressed, and sat down in the tub. J.D. walked in, grabbed the bucket of warm water off the wood stove, and poured it around her in the tub. Then he grabbed the soap and began to wash her back.

"Mae, tell me something, did you really mean what you said about one bull in the pasture? It sounded like you don't intend to let this revenge thing go. I want to spend more time with you. I think I may be falling for you, and I hope the feeling is mutual."

"Yes, J. D. What the hell does J. D. stand for anyway!"

"J. D. is short for Josiah Dirkland. It's an old family name."

Laughingly, Mae said, "Holy cow! How about I call you Jay?"

"Sure, that is fine. Now you never answered my question."

"Oh, that. Look, two men who were very important to me died due to incompetence by their commanders. They should be held accountable by someone. It's not fair."

"Don't worry, they will be held accountable. If not by the Army, then by themselves. I have led large numbers of men into combat. My first skirmish as a Captain, I was so shit scared, I could barely give the command to advance. War is chaos. There is no other way to describe it. As a Major, I commanded multiple companies. The decisions I made on the battlefield twisted my guts up inside. I had to perch myself on the high ground and watch my men attack the enemy in the valley below. Luckily, our artillery neutralized theirs, and we won the battle after a successful musket volley and bayonet charge. The next day, my men wiped out an entire company-sized element. For that, my unit received a battlefield commendation. Afterward, I was a favorite with the newspapers after they discovered the outcome. Major J. D. Malone, the Dandy Irishman, struck a mighty and decisive blow to the enemy. My men and I just did our jobs. Nothing else! No valiant speeches or sanctimonious bravado. Just men under extreme duress asked to perform a despicable task upon another group of soldiers, all of whom had families they desperately longed to reunite with. There would be no reunion for those men. The General ordered the Colonel, the Colonel ordered me, I ordered my Captains to show no quarter as they attacked."

Mae just sat there in the tub contemplating the words. Her grief could not justify adding to the ugliness of war and the psychological scars that never penetrate to the surface, only much later disseminating as demonic nightmares. Jay could see that her heart had softened to the idea of assassinating two fellow officers. She stifled herself in the resolve that those men would punish themselves long before she could.

Sunday morning found Ma, Jay, and the boys riding to an abandoned stagecoach outpost about ten miles south of Frisco. The perfect place to do some target practice.

"Okay, boys, let me see you shoot the bottles off that fence." Ten shots rang out, but all the bottles were left standing.

"Okay, I see this is going to be a long day. Go ahead and take the cylinders out of your pistols. Mae, take these pennies and lay them flat on top of the barrels. Okay, boys, go ahead and pull the trigger." Both pennies hit the ground. "Keep pulling the trigger until the pennies stay on the barrels." It took almost half an hour before they both could engage the trigger without the pennies falling off the barrels.

"Okay, reload with these cylinders. Fire when ready." Ten shots fired, ten bottles gone.

"Much better. That was lesson one. Lesson two, engage targets under fire." Two hours later, they could hit three out of five targets under fire.

"Lesson three, how to survive a firefight. Shoot and move. Don't let the enemy get a fix on your position after two shots; move to another location. Also, never pick a fight with a faster gun. They will kill you. you can practice drawing from your holster on your own. Just remember to remove the cylinder before you start, lest you shoot a hole in your foot. Well, that's all I got. Let's go home and get some supper.

Back home, Mae whipped up some eggs and bacon along with bread and butter. Mae spoils me, and I really appreciate it at times. After supper, I showed Andrew and Tommy how to properly clean their pistols. Afterward, Mae and I went upstairs to get ready for bed. We ended up sharing a bath together. As I sat back in the shared soapy bathwater, my thoughts wandered to the thought of marriage. I told myself several years ago I would not go looking for a wife again, but Mae touches my heart in much the same way my first wife did before I lost Andrea to an outlaw in the spring of 1858. After that, I had no interest in staying in Texas as a deputy sheriff. I figured it was time to move on.

California was still booming and starting to lose some of its initial lawlessness. I figured, why not head for Frisco? I was young enough that I could still make a decent living with my gun as a lawman or whatever. Hauling freight seemed safer than bounty hunting, and the hours were sure better. Now I find myself contemplating the "M" word again. I am not sure that Mae is ready for another husband just yet. I do find it puzzling with regard to how open Mae is when it comes to sex. I just assumed she would not be willing to partake in premarital relations due to her Quaker background. I was very much mistaken. Happily mistaken. I guess I may need to be patient with Mae and see where our relationship goes. It would appear she has strong feelings for me. I don't think she is just using me for a good poke every now and again. At least I hope not.

"Mae, do you miss Thomas very much. The reason I ask is because even now, I dwell on Andrea quite a bit."

"Jay, how long were you married before she died?"

"Three years."

"Any talk of children to that point?"

"We tried, but she never got pregnant. God's will, I guess."

"Jay, how many men have you killed?"

"Countless as an Army officer, fourteen as a lawman, and two in self-defense after being drawn upon. My reputation seemed to follow me no matter where I went."

"Any regrets?"

"Sure, not so much now, but back on active duty, I had more than a few sleepless nights. I would lie in my cot and stare up at the darkness above me. I would ask myself why all those men had to die. I don't think I will ever really know why men go to war, pride, religion, monetary gain, political ideals, who knows. All I can say at this point is my soldiering days are over. I have learned to accept my past, learn from it, and move on. Now my dreams are all about you and me together."

"You're a good man, J. D. Malone. I think about you a lot, too. My heart is happy right now. You are the reason for my happiness. I like what we have accomplished together here, and I hope we can grow with each other. The boys really like you. You are good for them. Those two were a bit troublesome back in Missouri, especially after their Pa was killed. Now they have someone to look up to again. Thank you for all that you do for them. I can usually handle them to a point, but sometimes we are too close to one another. Mothering becomes smothering. They need guidance from a non-family member in order for it to resonate."

"Sure, Mae, I am happy to mentor them in any way I can. Down deep, they are completely devoted to you, though they don't always show it. Sometimes I don't think you realize how conveniently rare a person you are. Once Tommy and Andrew get past all the barking and constant ordering them around, they know you love them both dearly. Sometimes that can get lost in the moment. That was the case with my mother as well. Unfortunately, she died giving birth to my sister. Ma was in her forties, and she expired minutes after the birth. My sister Mary died in an orphanage a week later. Pa wasn't there when they died. He didn't find out until almost two months later.

My Pa, Bruce Malone, was not a real family man in the traditional sense. He was a buffalo hunter and was almost never home. He was real good about sending money, though. Once a year or so, he would actually make it back home to our big cabin in Tennessee. That was usually during the spring thaw. Pa hated dealing with all that mud. Come May, he would be off again for ten months. He would be home just long enough to instruct me how to fix all the broken stuff on Ma's honey-do list. I can't really complain about Pa. He kept food on the table and taught me how to be resourceful. His connections as an Army scout were enough to get me a place at the Academy. The man had lots of friends, well-to-do and otherwise. I guess you could call him a wilderness ambassador. The man spoke Sioux, Cheyenne, Cherokee, and a few other native American languages. Some years, he would return home with as much as $1000 in cash. He usually gave all but $100 to Ma.

Ma, on the other hand, was the quintessential pioneer woman. She was strong, resourceful, and every bit as dangerous with a firearm as I am. Ma was always elated to see Pa return home and cried every time he left for the plains. Some years, I think she was ready to see Pa head back out before he was. About a month was all she could tolerate with that man. They did love each other in their own way. Wow, I have been talking up a storm here. We are both starting to prune from this bathwater. Let's dry off and go to bed." Mae stepped out of the tub first. Jay sat there looking at her slender and shapely female form. All the while thinking to himself how fortunate he was to be with such a beautiful and intelligent woman. She could probably have just about any man in San Francisco given her assets, so why me? He thought to himself, Don't ask such stupid questions, you know the answer. You make her life easier because of your reputation as a gunfighter. Just enjoy the time you have together. Later on, she may see through you, but for now, be happy in the moment.

"Are you coming to bed, handsome?"

"Be right there, sweetheart." We snuggled beside one another well into the night before falling asleep in each other's arms. I wonder if she really would marry me if I asked right now.

Chapter 6:
A Problem in Kansas

November 18, 1862. 0500 in Tamsford, Kentucky. Just moments before the officer's call, Major Luke Anderson makes his way to the General Bank's tent. The General begins his address.

"Good morning, gentlemen. Finally, we are in the thick of the war. This division is to capture the rail hub just outside of Tamsford, Kentucky. There are three enemy companies guarding the railhead, and they must be neutralized before we can successfully occupy the enemy depot. Colonel Bates' regiment will cover the right flank. Colonel Grier's regiment will attack on the left flank. Our artillery will fire directly upon theirs. Once their artillery has been sufficiently weakened, Major Anderson, your cavalry will attack directly from the north. As the retreating rebels advance south, the remaining regiment will capture what's left."

Luke spoke up, "General sir, would it not be more effective to have my Cavalry unit attack first and draw their attention away from the flanks prior to Colonel Grier's attack?"

"That will be quite enough, Major. Okay, men, you have your orders. Colonel Grier will attack at 0730, and the artillery barrage will begin at 0745. Good luck and God's speed in our victory."

Colonel Gage Grier and Luke were walking back to their company's assembly areas together. Once out of earshot of the command post, Sage spoke up, "Luke, this is a trap. There have been several reports of rebel reserves all over covering our flanks right now. When the old man was notified, he disregarded them, convinced that there weren't any reserves in the area. He is still under the impression that we are only going to engage one confederate regiment, not a whole division. All you have to do is look at their artillery and know that it is a division-sized element. General Banks is the biggest windbag, damn political appointee, and he doesn't know shit about tactics."

"Gee Gage, why don't you stop beating around the bush and say how you really feel?" Both men laughed.

"I agree with you, Banks is an idiot when it comes to tactics. He is very good with logistics, and that is where the Army should utilize him. I heard he got his field command through his buddy, the Governor of Ohio. Another damn politician. No matter how he got here, this battle is going to happen. I will see you after it is all over."

"Right. Luke, keep your head down."

Luke ordered his men to fall in and march out in a column of two. As ordered, he placed himself stealthily behind the enemy artillery to the north of their position.

"Corporal Proust."

"Yes, sir! Major sir!"

"Take three men and scout the location one mile to our southwest. Colonel Grier will be engaging from that direction. I suspect he is running straight into an ambush. Report back to me immediately."

"Yes, sir! Right away, sir." The small scouting party rode off and returned about ten minutes later.

"Corporal Proust reporting as ordered, sir."

"What is out there?"

"You were right, sir. A company of rebel infantry and cavalry are waiting to ambush their advance."

"Corporal, get a message to headquarters. Tell them Colonel Grier's left is exposed to ambush by two company-sized elements, one infantry and one cavalry. Breaking off to eliminate ambush. Major Anderson" Proust managed to proceed his way around to contact General Bank's staff.

"Corporal Proust with a message from Major Anderson, sir."

General Waters took the message to General Banks. Upon receiving the message, General Banks uttered to his staff, "If Major Anderson is not killed during the battle, have him arrested and confined to his quarters for exceeding my direct order."

General Waters spoke up, "General Sir, Colonel Grier is walking into an ambush. Major Anderson is attempting to eliminate that threat."

"Major Anderson is disregarding my direct order. I will hear no more of this incident."

"Yes, sir, nothing follows."

Luke placed his cavalry in close proximity between the two rebel companies. Colonel Grier was still out of range for the rebel infantry to engage. Luke then split his forces, attacking both companies simultaneously. Both rebel units were taken completely by surprise. The successful attack took only minutes to kill or capture both rebel companies. As Colonel Grier's Regiment advanced in preparation for the attack, they were surprised to find Major Anderson waiting for them with over a hundred captured enemy soldiers.

Major Anderson rode up to Colonel Grier and exclaimed, "Sir, please escort these prisoners of war to General Banks with my complements."

Major Anderson ordered his unit back to the position north of the enemy artillery in order to carry out his original mission. Colonel Bates Regiment encountered a company of rebel infantry while advancing upon their position, suffering over one hundred casualties, while driving the rebels out of their ambush position. The battle of Tamsford Depot was a huge Union victory due in large part to Major Anderson's excellent battlefield maneuver. However, Luke would not receive any credit for his masterful heroics. Immediately following the battle, Luke was placed under arrest pending a Court-Martial, charging Major Luke Anderson with insubordination and exceeding a direct order from a superior officer.

An official inquiry into the charges brought forth against Major Anderson concluded that he acted without orders and deliberately put himself and the entire division in danger by exceeding his orders and subsequently abandoning his post. Proceedings for a General Court Martial were to commence sixty days from this date on January 25, 1863.

Colonel Grier, out of gratitude for probably saving his life and the lives of many of his men during the battle in question, sent a telegram to Mae in San Francisco.

Mae was just about to close the store for lunch when Bill Nuberg came running over from the Telegraph office with a message all the way from Fort Hays, Kansas. She opened the envelope and read: Luke to be court martialed in fifty-eight days. Please come to Fort Hays, Kansas, as soon as possible.

Chapter 7:
Son in Crisis

Mae immediately went back into the store and began to pack her grip. When Tommy and Andrew came back from the warehouse, she told them to pack up their gear and meet her in the barn so they could get the wagon ready for the trip to Fort Hays.

Jay walked into the room. "Why are you going to Fort Hays?"

"Luke is being court martialed, and we are going out there right now. If you are coming with us, you better get your stuff and saddle your horse. Then meet us in the barn." Mae and the boys got the wagon ready to move out. then they grabbed two months' worth of rations. Jay met them in the barn.

Jay asked, "Mae, what are you going to do with the store?"

"I am going to sell everything down to the last plug of chewing tobacco to the bank. Arnold Gray over at the bank has been trying to partner with me ever since I showed up here. He will be more than happy to take the store and all the inventory off my hands." The four of them headed straight for the bank and barged right into Arnold's office. Thirty minutes later, Mae walked out of the bank with $9000. The next stop was the gun shop. Mae bought four brand new Spencer rifles, eight pistols, and a crapload of ammo.

"Jay, here is a new rifle for you. I assume you know how to use it. God willing, it should take about a month to get to Fort Hays."

Jay interjected, "Mae, you look like you are ready to start a war."

"If that is what it is going to take to get Luke out of jail, so be it." Then she hoisted herself up in the wagon, grabbed the reins, and yelled, "Yah mules, Yah!" and they were on their way back to Kansas.

The four of them ended up taking the southern route through El Paso. Every night, Jay would try and convince Mae that this was not the way to go about this.

"Sweetheart, why don't you let me try and telegram some of my friends in Washington, D. C.? I am still well thought of back east."

"Look, Jay, this is a family thing. I have to do this my way."

"Mae, at this point, we don't even know what Luke is charged with. At least let me send a wire to Fort Hays and find out what the story is."

"No, we will be there in ten days, according to the stage driver we talked to yesterday."

"Mae Anderson, you are a stubborn woman."

"Yes, and I am not going to change any time soon. So, mount up and just enjoy the trip."

"Okay, Mae, but this is not going to end the way you think it is." After twelve days, we finally arrived at Fort Hays. We introduced ourselves to the perimeter guard as friends and family of Major Anderson. The officer of the day let us in, and we were escorted to the command post. We were given an audience with the Executive Officer, General Foster."

He spoke up, "Mrs. Anderson, gentlemen, J. D., what can I do for you?"

"Well, for starters, you can tell me why my son is under attest."

"Madam, Major Anderson is being detained pending the outcome of his court-martial."

"And what pray tell, are the charges?"

"I am afraid I can't discuss military matters with civilians."

At the top of her voice, she ranted, "You can't discuss military matters with..." J. D. pulled her back from the general's desk and said, "Calm down, Mae! General, we just traveled over a thousand miles to find out what the hell is going on. Surely you can dispense with protocol given the situation."

"Very well. Your son is being charged with insubordination, failure to follow a direct order, and exceeding his orders."

J. D. asked, "General, what happened?"

"Look, folks, technically he exceeded his orders, and because he did, an entire Union regiment is alive today."

Mae intervened, "Who filed the charges?"

"General Banks, our division commander."

"May we have a word with him?"

"No, ma'am."

"Can we at least see my son?"

"Yes, I will allow you to visit with him briefly. As long as you agree to follow our instructions while doing so."

"Agreed."

Ma led the group to the brig. Immediately after entering, they were searched for weapons. The Sergeant was surprised to find Mae's sawed-off shotgun sewn in the lining of her petticoat. She told him it was for snakes and serpents. We walked down the corridor to the cell Luke was being held in. The guard stood by after allowing us to enter his cell. Mae asked the guard how long it had been since he had eaten any real meat. She produced a nice hunk of fresh bacon from her apron. "Maybe you could find a nice quiet place to eat this while we get reacquainted with my son."

"Yes, ma'am, take all the time you need." The guard walked back down the corridor and sat quietly.

Mae started off, "How the hell do you manage to save an entire regiment of men and end up in the brig for it?"

"General Banks, that's how." Luke proceeded to give the four of us a detailed account of the incident. "The court-martial is slated to begin in three weeks. General Banks is going to preside over it personally."

J. D. quipped, "Why does the general have it in for you?"

"Mostly because I have a set of balls and question him on tactics during officer calls. Beyond that, I don't know. How did you find out I was here?"

"Colonel Grier sent me a telegram."

"Gage sent word to you. He's a good man. Sean Foster is, too."

Mae asked, "What can we do to stop Banks from throwing you in prison?"

"Nothing! The most I should get is a few years. I can try and fight it on appeal. Hopefully, my case finds a sympathetic ear in the War Department. My legal counsel, Lt. Harris, thinks I should change my plea to guilty and throw myself on the mercy of General Banks."

"I have a better idea, sonny boy. You just sit tight until the court martial. In the meantime, here is some bacon and a biscuit. I will try and get some real food to you from now on."

"Ma, don't do anything stupid, okay?" Mae, J. D., and the boys left the fort and set up camp about a mile outside the fort entrance. Every evening, soldiers would bring prairie hens for Mae to cook for them. Soon, she had quite a following with the enlisted men.

Everyone suspected what she was up to, but there was no way in hell to prove it.

J. D. was able to reacquaint himself with an old friend stationed at Fort Hays, Sgt. Maj. Riley, who was a corporal in J.D.'s unit during the Mexican-American War. They had much to talk about weeks before Luke's kangaroo court started. Turns out nobody can stand General Banks. All the enlisted men think he is a pompous, arrogant ass, and they really don't like having him in charge prior to the tribunal.

"J. D., this is Sean Foster's command, and Banks has no business superseding Foster like this. Don't quote me on this, but I think Banks is the one who should be facing a court-martial. The man has us running around whitewashing rocks for Pete's sake."

"I thought this place was awful pretty for a frontier outpost."

"That ain't the half of it. He took away our whiskey ration. That didn't sit well with the men, I'll tell you. Beer, that is all the spirits you will find on this fort. It's warm to boot. A sad way to run an Army if you ask me. We should be out chasing down those Missouri Raider's. What do we do, sweep porches and paint rocks all day?"

"So, most of the men here don't like Banks. Are there any men that do?"

"Major Miles and Captain Jenkins are on the general's staff and arrived with him a week after Major Anderson. If you ask me, the man is getting the raw end of it. Luke Anderson is the real deal. He is probably the best horseman I have ever met. Sgt. West says he can hit any target at a full gallop, day or night. Now look at him. He's rotting away in the brig because some lame ass general got shown up during a battle. Banks ought to be licking the Major's boots for securing the victory. Not to mention saving that entire regiment.

J.D. I'm drunk, or as drunk as I can get on this stuff. I'm going to hit the hay."

"Sarge, just suppose, if you could. Would you be willing to turn the tables on General Banks?"

"Just between you, me, and that dirty spittoon, yes, I would. What do you need me to do, or not do, in this case? Are you thinking of springing the Major? Well, the best time would be at the court-martial. No one would see that coming."

"Keep it under your bandanna, I'll see you later."

J. D. headed back to the wagon for supper. More prairie hens. It certainly beats hard tac. The soldiers were starting to head back to the fort after extra helpings of Mae's dumplings. J. D. and Mae sat down to supper with the boys.

Mae asked Jay, "So, what is the scuttlebutt around camp tonight?"

"I think we can count on a good portion of the enlisted men to help us. None of them gives a damn about General Banks. My Friend, Sgt.Maj. Riley, is all in. He despises the man. How Gen. Banks got so unpopular so fast is a mystery, but I am not going to look a gift horse in the mouth. Tommy, Andrew, you are going to have to detain the general's aides. You will need to restrain them during the court-martial. That's when we break Luke out. Go to their office and tell them you want to enlist. Then gag and tie them up back-to-back against one another and shove them in a closet. Mae, let's clean up the camp and take a walk."

"Sure, honey, what did you have in mind?" They walked hand in hand, watching the dusk disappear from the horizon.

"Mae. I don't know what side Sean Foster is on in this caper. I know he resents having his command swept away from him for no apparent reason. You are going to have to approach him. He is a widower. So, I'm guessing you will have better luck than I will getting through to him. I would not tell him of our plan to spring Luke out of the brig. He is not stupid; if you flirt with him, he will know you're up to something. I would tell him you would do anything to get Luke reinstated to his former assignment."

"Anything?"

"That's what I said. And you are really going to have to be convincing."

"Well, the man is not unattractive, and if I have your blessing, I will give the man a poke if I have to."

"Mae, you know we are going to be on the run after we pull this off right. Our next stop is Mexico or Canada. We can't stay in the U.S."

"I know. Canada is more to my liking. I grew up on the Hudson River. Montreal is beautiful. Cold but beautiful. Toronto is a bit closer."

"Mae, if you were to marry me, we could give false names on the marriage license. All we have to do is find a Justice of the peace between here and Canada."

"Jay, you would be willing to do that for me."

"Yes. I don't want to see Luke get railroaded by Gen. Banks either. Oh yeah, and another thing, I happen to be madly in love with you."

"Even if I have to share a bed with General Foster?"

"Yes, even after that. I hope you won't need to, though."

"Do you think now would be a good time to call on Gen. Foster?"

"Yes, you should pay the man a visit tonight."

"Okay, Jay, I will ride up there as soon as I get a little dolled up." The two of them embraced, standing alone in the darkness. Things were being put in motion that could not be stopped, even if they wanted to. Mae painted her face, slipped into her best dress, mounted her horse, and hurried off to Fort Hays to pay an unannounced visit to Gen. Foster. Once arriving at the fort, she was greeted by the century. A little bacon and biscuits got her an audience with Sean Foster. "Come in, Mrs. Anderson. To what do I owe this unexpected visit? Where are my manners? Please have a seat in the parlor. Would you care for a drink? Lemonade, or something stronger?"

"Whiskey, thank you. I am a little parched."

"I assume this is not a social call."

"Well, General, let's refer to this as a semi-social call and see where it leads. I am hoping that you have at least some influence with Gen. Banks. Sean, can I call you Sean?"

"Yes, please do, Mae, is it?"

"Yes, Sean, you must know I would do anything within my power to get Luke out of this jam he has gotten himself into. So that's why I am here, ready to barter for Luke's reinstatement. You know very well this upcoming trial is a farce from beginning to end. Why are you letting this happen?"

"Orders. I was instructed to temporarily relinquish my entire command to Banks and his staff until the conclusion of the, for lack of better words, kangaroo court."

"So, you agree Luke's actions were necessary given the situation he was in."

"Absolutely, upon your son's arrival, I only had him on restriction, not occupying a cell in the brig. That was Bank's doing. After reading the statement from Colonel Grier, I was shocked that

Luke was being brought up on charges. Unfortunately, at this point, my hands are tied. There will be an Adjutant General arriving any day now to begin preparing the tribunal. Believe me, I wish I had the authority to put an end to this nonsense."

"Sean, may I impose upon you for another drink? You know the scuttlebutt around camp is that Luke is being railroaded by a completely incompetent ass, in General Banks. In fact, there are only two other men on this post who agree with the General."

"Yes, I am well aware of that fact." Mae stood up and began to loosen her blouse, claiming the whiskey had made her uncomfortably warm. Then she waltzed over to Sean and placed her hands in his, leaned forward and whispered in his ear, "I don't suppose there is any way I could untie your hands in this matter."

"Mae, all I can do right now is have another discussion with Bank's, but I feel that it is pointless."

"Sean, I feel the need to lie down. Is there a bed in this place where I can rest?" After a lengthy bit of seduction, Sean was not opposed to giving General Banks a piece of his mind.

The next morning, Sean awoke after a very satisfying night's sleep, got dressed, and made a beeline to his old office, which was now occupied by Gen. Banks.

He knocked on the office door. "Come in, Sean."

"General Foster to see the General Sir."

"At ease, Sean. Okay, let's hear it."

"Sir, you can't really go through with this. You know as well as I do that the Major made the right call. You never would have successfully completed your mission without the help of Major Anderson. You should be commending him, not punishing him like this. Put your ego aside just this once and do the right thing. Sir, you know damn well this is going to be overturned at appeal, or the charges will be reduced at the very least."

"Sean, I know he made the right call. I just didn't like the way he went about it. It was very unprofessional. "You are going to ruin a man's career because of one sarcastic remark."

"Yes, I am!"

"Permission to speak freely, sir?"

"Go ahead."

"You are really an arrogant ass, and you are going to regret this. I hope this costs you your command. I hear your executive officer, General Waters, is doing a hell of a job in your absence. Maybe the deed is already done."

"That's enough, or I will have you disciplined for insubordination too."

"Very well, I apologize if any of my statements offended thee, Sir. Permission to retire, sir."

"Get out of my sight." Sean left the office and rode out to see Mae at her camp.

J. D. welcomed Sean to the camp. Sean dismounted and greeted everyone. J. D. handed him a fresh cup of coffee. "Can I add a little hair of the dog with it, sir?"

"Yes, thank you. Call me Sean from now on. That arrogant ass. There is no chance of the General dropping the charges. All I can do at this point is sponsor a dance the night before the tribunal in honor of the Adjutant and get everyone severely hungover for the morning of. I still have to maintain all watches by the book. Do me a personal favor and kidnap that son of a bitch in broad daylight. Get him the hell off my post. I don't care what you do with those two brown nosing aides of his." General Foster finished his coffee and rode back to Fort Hays.

Mae spoke up, "Damn, everybody hates that son of a bitch. Ok. Andrew, you and Tommy will subdue the General's aides. Don't shoot them, just tie them up and gag them. Jay and I will do the rest in the courtroom. We are going to need six fresh mounts."

Jay said, "SgtMaj. Riley will take care of that. We still have ten days until the trial. We need to put the camp at ease with our presence. Mae, you have been taking Luke's lunch every day. Why don't you start taking him meals twice a day? Meanwhile, I will start losing at poker. The end of the month is in two days. The enlisted men will already be starting to take markers for payday. Everybody loves a pigeon. Let's just hope that General Banks doesn't figure out he's being played. How are the rations holding up?" Mae responded, "Plenty of flour, sugar, corn, and sow belly. I could feed half the camp for another week at least, and there are no shortages of prairie hens around." Jay asked Andrew, "How about weapons and ammo?"

"Right now we have over a thousand Spencer rounds, a full ten-pound keg of black powder, seven topped-off powder horns, over five thousand caps, over twelve hundred pistol balls, four Spencer rifles, and twelve pistols."

"Good. Let's go ahead and start setting up five possible bags. We can carry the bulk Spencer cartridges on our gun belts and saddlebags. We're going to need bunk rolls also. I'll see if Riley can help us with those. Okay, everyone, gather around." J. D. started mapping out a plan to kidnap the General and get out of Fort Hays alive. "First of all, do not kill any soldier stationed at Fort Hays. If that happens, we will never get out alive. We go in the morning of the tribunal together in the covered wagon. The rifles stay in the wagon. Everyone will carry a pistol under their coat, except Ma, with her sawed-off shotgun. After we take our seats in the courtroom, Tommy and Andrew will head for the General's office to subdue the aides. You need to return as soon as you can to help cover our escape from the courtroom with General Banks. As soon as the Generals enter the room, we have to get the drop on everyone. Four guns should do it. Mae, you lay both barrels on banks, and I will come up behind and escort him out the door first. Andrew, you cover the rear. Tommy, you hop in the wagon and roll the team around to the headquarters entrance. I will put Banks in the wagon, and we will ride out together, all six of us. Once we clear the main gate, we need to get out of rifle range fast. If the centuries don't know Banks is with us, we should be okay. Then we head for our staging area five miles north. The terrain will cover up our escape. At that location, we are completely out of sight of the Fort. Then we dump off Banks, mount our horses, and haul ass to Canada. That's if everything goes exactly the way we planned it."

Mae interjected, "What if there are complications and we have to shoot our way out?"

"Then we are probably all dead. If we can convince everyone on that post that we pose no threat to them, we have a real good chance at pulling this off. Remember, there will be a big dance the night before the trial. That means lots of booze and drunk soldiers. Honestly, I like our chances. Speaking of booze, how much whiskey do we have left?"

Tommy crawled into the wagon and said, "We are down to two cases."

"Good, we will bring it to the dance."

So, for the next nine days, the four of them spent a good amount of time at the fort doing lots of horse trading with the soldiers. Ma doubled up on meals for Luke. She would purposely show up between meals with biscuits and sow's belly. She was starting to build up quite a fan base. If I didn't know any better, I would say she was born to spy work. The way she managed to build relationships with everyone in the camp. The centuries didn't even bother challenging her anymore. They couldn't get their hands on a fresh biscuit fast enough. The camp mess sergeant was no match for Ma. He even asked her for a few recipes. General Banks was rarely seen outside of his office and living quarters. The man didn't even attend roll call. It was as if he was just biding his time until the Adjutant General Arrived. General Banks would receive telegraphs containing orders from the War Department. They were disregarded. He had no interest at all in taking part in the war effort.

That all changed the minute that Adjutant General Wise arrived at Fort Hays three days prior to the trial. Everything from that point forward was by the book and dressed right. Surprisingly, Ma, J. D., and the boys were still permitted on the base. Even Gen. Foster was puzzled at that. Amazingly enough, Luke was released from the brig and placed on restriction until the court-martial convened. General Wise was not one bit pleased that a fellow officer was subject to such harsh treatment for a non-capital charge.

Then came the eve of Luke's tribunal. As promised, there was a post-wide dance held to welcome General Wise. The procession was open to enlisted men and officers alike. Dress uniforms required. The other soldiers helped themselves to the two cases of whiskey provided by Ma and J.D. over in the canteen. There were a lot of boilermakers put away that night. So far, everything was falling into place nicely.

All the preparations made by J. D. and Ma were in place. Even the fresh horses staged five miles north of Fort Hays just before dawn. Three hours until Zulu time. The countdown has begun.

Chapter 8:
Justice for Luke

8:00 am, time to take the wagon into Fort Hays. Ma, J. D., Andrew, and Tommy climbed aboard. When they arrived, the front gate swung wide open to let them pass, completely unaware of the hidden chaos that was about to unfold. Once inside, Ma passed out brunch to the enlisted soldiers gathered around her by the wagon. J. D. quicky met with SgtMaj. Riley. They headed over to the telegraph room. Riley distracted the men on duty while J. D. severed the wire, then headed over to the courtroom. He walked into the courtroom to find Ma, and the boys were the only ones there. A few minutes later, Luke was escorted in by four armed guards. Immediately, Andrew and Tommy scampered over to the command post to subdue the General's aides. Tommy walked through the door. Major Miles and Captain Jenkins were sitting at their desks, shuffling through paperwork. The Major spoke up, "What can I do for you boys this morning?"

Tommy drew his pistol and announced, "Shut up, gentlemen, and get your hands in the air." Andrew started tying the two men back-to-back and placed handkerchiefs in their mouths, then shuffled them into the closet and jammed a chair under the doorknob. Andrew pulled the shades three-quarters down over the window. Both boys calmly and casually returned to the courtroom. As Tommy sat down, he gave Ma a wink. Approximately five minutes later, the Sgt. of the Guard announced, "Attention." Everyone who was seated stood up as the three generals entered the room. General Banks ordered everyone to take their seats. Just as General Banks slammed his gavel on the table to start the procession, Ma, J. D., and the boys drew their weapons and got the drop on the entire room. General Banks spoke up and said, "What is the meaning of this?" Ma told him, "General Banks, you are coming with us." Almost immediately, General Wise stood up and reached for his sidearm. J. D. struck him in the back of the head with his .44 pistol. Wise hit the floor. The boys grabbed the rifles from the guards and unlocked Luke's handcuffs. J. D. handed Luke his spare pistol. Ma announced, "Anybody follows us out of this room and the General gets both barrels in the back of the head." The five of them escorted the general out the door and up into the back of the wagon. Tommy drove the rig right out the front gate, then raised the team to a full gallop. The Sgt. of the Guard came out of the courtroom and yelled, "Stop them, they kidnapped the general!" Rifle shots rang out from the centuries. One round caught Andrew in the upper back. Ma grabbed him up and hugged him. At this point, Andrew was already spitting up lots of blood.

Ma screamed, "No, not my little Andrew. She started crying, sobbing uncontrollably. Then the crying suddenly stopped. Ma looked straight into the General's eyes and uttered, "General, you are a dead man." She sat back and placed Andrew's dead body on the floor of the wagon, cocked both barrels of her sawed-off shotgun, and just stared at General Banks. He uttered, "Mrs. Anderson, this is not my fault." Ma retorted, "Like hell it ain't!" Tommy pulled the wagon to a halt. They arrived at the staging area, transferred the remaining gear to the mules, and escorted General Banks out of the wagon. Ma said, "Now, General Kenneth Banks, strip off that uniform." The man started to undress and said, "Killing me won't solve anything."

"Shut up and get that damn uniform off." The man stood next to his uniform in his long johns. "Strip off those long johns, too." He complied, standing in the middle of a large plain, completely flushed with any dignity. "Now raise your hands high." Boom! Ma emptied both barrels in his chest. Whatever notions of a peaceful solution to Luke's military complications just ended. Now, the four of them were truly on the run. The body count now stands at four, and it is a good bet that the number was going to increase.

Moments prior, the centuries watched as the wagon rode completely out of sight. SgtMaj Riley muttered to himself, "Damn if they didn't pull it off. There's going to be hell to pay around here when Washington learns of this." Riley called a meeting of his senior NCOs immediately. The meeting was held in the brig. "Gentlemen, take a good look around. If we don't come up with a plan to admonish ourselves of this fiasco, this is where we can count on living for some time. Fortunately, we have a scapegoat in General Kenneth Banks. He was so lax with security around here, a Sunday School Class could have robbed this place blind. Just remember this during your testimony at the investigation. Tell them, 'We were under direct orders from General Banks, Sir.' As long as we stick together, it won't matter what those boot-licking aides of his claim. By the way, has anybody seen them lately? Buzz, go check on them."

"Right away, Sgt. Maj." Buzz walked into the Major's office and heard grumbling from the closet. He opened the door to witness a very comical sight. The two of them tied back-to-back. He immediately removed the handkerchiefs from their mouths and cut off their bindings. "Sgt. Buzz, what the hell happened?"

"General Banks has been kidnapped." All three men scurried outside. The post was immediately put on alert. General Foster dispatched a telegram to Washington for further instructions, only to be informed that the line is down. "How is General Wise?" The corpsman informed General Foster that he was still unconscious. It could be a while before General Wise starts to regain consciousness." "Very well, take him to my quarters and see to his injury."

"Yes, sir." General Foster thought to himself, at least I have my command back. "Lt. Barnes, send out a detail to see where the telegraph is cut. Also, take your platoon and pick up the Anderson's trail."

"Right away, sir." The lieutenant returned from the patrol hours later without securing telegraph communications and having to report the discovery of General Banks' remains. "It was a shotgun blast that killed him, sir. We found him." pause, "Stripped naked, lying next to his uniform. We also discovered Tommy Anderson's dead body lying in the abandoned wagon, sir. The gang transferred to horses and headed northeast. I don't believe they doubled back. At least not yet, sir. Right now, I would say they have about a six-hour start on us. It would appear their destination is Canada, sir."

SgtMaj. Riley reported. "The telegraph wire is repaired, sir. It was severed in the communications room sometime between 2000 hrs. yesterday and now, sir. That was when the last message was received. We will never be able to identify the individual who cut the wire. It could have happened during the party, sir."

"That will be all Sgt. Maj. Riley. Return to your post."

"Sir, yes, sir." General Foster walked to the communications room and had a wire sent to his Corps Commander, Major General Graves.

General Banks kidnapped and found dead on the plain. Persons of interest: Mae Anderson, J. D. Malone, Major Luke Anderson, U.S.A., Tommy Anderson. Probable destination, Canada. Please advise.

Six hours later, General Foster received instructions not to investigate and that the matter was now under the direct jurisdiction of the War Department. Upon receiving the telegram, General Foster placed an officer call where he instructed his staff not to subdue or investigate the matter further in any way. The Adjutant, General Wise, after recovering from his injury, returned to his post forthwith.

Chapter 9:
No Accountability

Two months on the lam in Toronto, Canada, and no repercussions whatsoever from the U.S. Army or any law enforcement agency.

There wasn't even a warrant out on Luke for desertion. Mae began to hypothesize that if no one knew why General Banks was killed, then Andrew's death was for no reason. Mae announced, "No, no, they are not going to cover this up. We are going to knock off a few more generals. That should get someone to start taking notice."

Jay intervened, "Mae, do you know what you are saying. The four of us managed to pull off the perfect crime, and you want to knock off more generals just to draw some headlines. Do you even hear what you're saying?"

"Oh yes, I think I know exactly what I am saying, those bastards buried my husband and two of my sons. I want somebody to be held accountable."

"What are you going to do, Mae, assassinate every general in the war department and the Secretary of War?"

"No, damn you, just the incompetent bastards that got my Thomas and John killed."

"Mae, this is insane! The fact that we kidnapped, killed Kenneth Banks, and got away with it was a miracle. Now you want to add two more to the body count."

"Yes, that's right, I do, because we have to put an end to the subordinate chaos."

"Okay. You want to tell me how we are going to kill two generals, each surrounded by an entire division of men?"

"Don't you know, the same way we did it before, we infiltrate the camp, kidnap, and execute them. Only this time we leave a calling card."

"Mae, you are forgetting one thing: General Crawford was killed in the same battle as Thomas."

"I want to assassinate the Corp Commanders also. Then we surely get noticed. Look, you said yourself most of these senior field officers are clueless, especially the political appointees. I want them to suffer like all the other mothers burying an empty coffin on their family farms. I would have had three on mine alone."

"Mae, this is not going to stop the war. It may prolong it. I, for one, do not want any part of this."

"You don't have a choice. You are a member of the Scattergun Mae Anderson Gang. In for a penny, in for a pound. If we have to, we can call ourselves a militia and recruit more volunteers in our cause. The way I see it, we are just assassinating high-ranking officers who had a major hand in the death of my immediate family members. I am declaring war on the men who killed my husband and sons."

"This is so crazy it is starting to make sense. Okay, I'm all in. Who do we go after next?"

"General Archibald Mendalbine. He was General Crawford's commander."

"How did you find that out?"

"Major Miles told me back at Fort Hays. He said this guy is a real dumbass."

"Okay, the easiest way to find this guy is by talking to a newspaper reporter. It's late and I'm tired. I am going to bed. Do you want to come with me?"

"No. I am going to stay up for a while if that's okay."

"Sure, sweetheart. Good night." That was the last time J. D. would see Mae or Luke for quite some time. She and the boys lit out shortly after J. D. fell asleep. Mae left $500.00 on the nightstand. I guess it was her way of thanking him for all the kindness he had shown toward Mae and her family.

J. D. woke up early the next morning, finding himself alone in the two-bedroom suite that the four of them had shared for over a month. He quickly got dressed, pocketed the money left for him, and scurried downstairs to enquire about transferring to a smaller room for the duration of his stay in the hotel. The concierge informed him that a single suite had already been paid for in his name for the next two weeks. Then J. D. was handed a message from Mae.

My dearest love,

I guess this is where we part ways. Thank you for all the love, affection, and kindness that you brought to my family and I. I sincerely wish that we could have met under different circumstances. You are a good and honorable man. I consider myself very fortunate to have loved you during the time we spent together.

It would appear, after last night's conversation, that you don't approve of my decision to escalate the issue I have with the U.S. Army right now. That being the case, I feel it would be better for everyone if the two of us separate and move on to engage our own interests at this time.

Please know that I will always keep the love we shared close to my heart for many days to come. I realize that the path I have chosen for

After reading the letter, J. D. headed right for the hotel saloon, only to find it did not open for another hour. He went back to the check-in counter and asked the concierge where the nearest open saloon was. The man looked over at the grandfather clock and saw it was 10:58 am. "Sir, the saloon next door will open in two minutes. Ours opens at noon and offers free meat sandwiches from noon to 1 pm. If you are interested. J. D. headed right next door."

The "Broken Rein Saloon" was completely empty of patrons when he walked in. J. D. sat down and ordered a bottle of whiskey and a cigar. He proceeded to light his cigar and puff away until the end was cherry red, then took the letter and burned it in the ashtray. He sat quietly and sipped several shots. The bartender came over and asked J. D. if he wanted to talk about it. "My woman just walked out on me before I had a chance to say goodbye. I guess she did me a favor, but it doesn't make it any easier."

"I assume that was the Dear John letter you burned up in the ashtray. They call me Big Hank."

"J. D. Malone, nice to meet you, sir."

"Irish J. D. Malone?"

"That's me."

"What brings you way up here? I thought you hailed from Texas."

"I came up here to get away from things for a while. Now my former girl has decided to leave me here and head back to the United States without me. We had a disagreement concerning ideology."

"Well, you couldn't have picked a better place to be right now, with the Union and the Confederacy still at each other's throats. I am originally from Maryland. I spotted the writing on the wall with the passing of the 'Missouri Compromise.' That's when I sold the three taverns I owned in Baltimore and relocated up here. Say, you wouldn't be interested in working as a bouncer here, would you? I could pay you one percent of the profits every week. Usually, thirty to forty bucks a week. It doesn't look like it now, but at night this place is jumping. My last bouncer ran off to California with one of the local barmaids. He said they were going to strike it rich in the gold country out west."

"I just came from San Francisco, and that place is full of penniless millionaires. In fact, my girl sold her general store before we headed back east. She cleared a very nice profit for herself. Almost 300%. That is where the money is, panning equipment and booze. I'm sure you are well aware of that. I think I might be interested. My hotel room is paid up for the next two weeks. I can certainly afford to stay that long. Thank you, I would like to come work for you very much."

"You can start just as soon as you sober up. I don't allow my people to drink on duty."

"I will be happy to oblige. My girl Mae, that is her name, she threw me for a loop. I think you just saved me an ugly hangover tomorrow morning. What time should I come back to start?"

"On a weekday like this, 7 pm sharp."

"Good, that will allow me time to clean up and sober up. I will see you at 7 pm sharp."

J. D. headed back to his suite and lay down for a bit to sleep off his inebriated state. He was actually a bit excited about the job. Rousting drunks was about all he ever did as a lawman down in Texas. A glance at the wall clock showed it was 6:45 pm. Time for work. He arrived five minutes early to see the place at almost half capacity. Beer and whiskey were flying up and down everywhere. Big Hank informed J. D. of the characters to watch out for. Everything went fairly smoothly, but it was a weeknight. The weekends could get much rowdier and usually more intense. Luckily, all the patrons were unarmed. Once everyone found out who the new bouncer was, the customers became a lot less frisky, as it were. J. D. never liked to talk about it, but he actually shot and killed the El Paso Tornado, Eli Duncan, an outlaw credited with killing fourteen men in a pistol showdown. It is the reason he left Texas in the first place. After that altercation, "Irish J. D. Malone" was the man with the fast gun that no one could or would want to challenge. California was supposed to be a way of escaping all that drama. Unfortunately, His reputation was ingrained in every cowboy's mind. J. D. Malone was the man to beat. Mae was all too thrilled to hire his freight company. Who the hell was going to be dumb enough to try to rob him? In Toronto, J. D. may finally have found a place where his reputation with a pistol could actually do some good.

Chapter 10:
Elizabeth

Two weeks went by quickly. J. D. was beginning to take on a celebrity status. Customers were starting to come in from all over Canada and the U.S. border states just to meet him.

"Hank, I am really kind of taken aback by all this hoopla concerning me and my shooting ability."

"Look, partner, I wouldn't worry about it too much. Eventually, it will start to die down some. Try and enjoy the attention. You have your choice of girls now."

"I know, and I am not really over Mae at this point. I find it hard to be sincere when most of the women I meet just want me for my physical presence, nothing any deeper."

"J. D., I will never figure you out, man. I'm sorry, but I would be all over these women. Like ducks on a Junebug. Like syrup on a flapjack. Like…"

"I get it. You would be all over them. Okay. The fact remains, I'm still stuck on Mae. That is going to take some time for me to bury that heartache. Especially since I can't drown my broken heart in liquor. I know, I know that's really not the answer."

"Not for nothing, man, but it has always been my observation that one day soon, a woman is going to come walking through those swinging doors and make you swoon all over her. Just give it a little time. Men have very short memories when it comes to affairs of the heart. You are doing fine. Just don't fall apart on me, okay?"

"Can do, thanks." As fate would have it, about three weeks later, a woman came in on the noon stage from Montreal, looking for someone to fix a broken strap on her left shoe. J. D. offered,

"Miss, I would be glad to escort you down the street to one of our blacksmiths. It is just down the street, the third building on the left."

"I don't want to impose, but that would be lovely if you could help me with this."

"It would be my pleasure, ma'am. Right this way." J.D. escorted her down the walkway to the Main Street Livery Stable." Once inside, J. D. called out, "Bruce, are you here?"

"Be right there." Half a minute passed. "Hi, J. D. Who is your lovely friend?"

"Oh, I don't know, I forgot to introduce myself. J. D. Malone at your service."

"J. D. Malone, the gunfighter?"

Bruce quipped, "Oh, for Pete's sake, is there anyone who hasn't heard of you?"

"I guess not. Yes, I am that J. D. Malone. May I ask your name?"

"Elizabeth M. Thomas, lovely to make your acquaintance."

Bruce asked, "Miss Thomas, how can I be of service to you today?"

"A strap on my shoe has broken off, and I would like to have this repaired."

"Piece of cake, I have almost the exact matching suede material available. It shouldn't take more than ten to fifteen minutes. Can I offer you a chair while I fix this for you?"

"Yes, thank you, Bruce. So, you are the famous J. D. Malone. Your picture doesn't do you credit."

"Where did you see my picture? I don't recall ever being photographed."

"It was a sketch of you in a New York City newspaper. The article was describing the gunfight between you and the El Paso Tornado."

"Oh, that, not my proudest moment. I just happened to walk into that saloon at the wrong time, or the right time, however you look at it."

"You really gunned him down in a draw right?"

"Yes, I did. I was lucky; he had just drunk two shots of whiskey before he drew around and tried to kill me. I still wonder to this day if I would have survived the encounter had he been completely sober."

"How much time elapsed between the time he drank those two shots and when he drew down on you?"

"It couldn't have been more than a minute or two."

"You would have definitely survived. He wasn't drunk yet."

"How do you know?"

"My father is a physician, and I am a nurse."

"Can I ask you another question? Why are you here?"

"I am checking in on my grandmother. She lives on the outskirts of Toronto. I was on my way there when the strap broke." Bruce walked back.

"Speaking of that, the repair is done."

"It's perfect. What do I owe you?"

"Half a dollar should do it."

"Thank you, Bruce." She handed him the payment and headed out the front of the stable.

"My pleasure, miss."

"J. D., you must come over to the house and meet my grandmother. She will be beside herself to meet you in person. She reads Western novels all the time. Oh, Grandma would have kittens. Will you come with me and introduce yourself?"

"Sure, I would be glad to meet your grandmother." J. D. borrowed a horse and buggy from Big Hank, and the two of them rode out to Grandma Thomas' place about five miles out of town. It was a grand three-story home with many gables."

"Elizabeth, her home is beautiful."

"I love it. I was born in this house. Sadly, my mother died giving birth to me. My Dad and Grandmother raised me in this house. My Dad has two offices. One in Montreal and another here in Toronto." J.D. followed Elizabeth up the steps to the entrance of the house and opened the door.

"Gramma, I'm here, and I brought a friend with me."

"Very good, dear. Who is your friend?" Gramma walked into the foyer and saw who Elizabeth brought with her. "J. D. Malone, as I live and breathe. Come in. Sit! Sit! Elsie, bring cookies and lemonade. Or would you prefer something stronger?"

"No, ma'am, lemonade would be perfect." Gramma parked herself right next to J. D. on the settee. Then she slipped her hand over his knee, touching his inner thigh. J. D. raised her hand and placed it gently back in her lap. "Well, you're no fun at all. I may as well let you court Lizzie over here."

"Gramma, please."

"Little girl, I ain't had this much man in the house for as long as I can remember. I am definitely taking a shot at him. Maybe he's into mature women."

"I would, but at this point, I'm not sure I would survive the honeymoon."

"Who said anything about marriage? Honeymoons are for virgins anyway. All those rose petals and moonbeams."

"Grammy, you are embarrassing the man." Elsie brought in the lemonade and cookies.

J. D. commented, "Elsie, these look delicious."

"Don't change the subject, stud. Oh, go ahead, have a cookie."

"Thank you, Ms. Thomas."

"Call me Kay, that's what all my former lovers called me."

"Kay, you are not going to give up, are you?"

"Nope, eat your cookie. By the way, how did you two meet?"

"I lost a strap on one of my shoes, and J. D. escorted me to the nearest blacksmith. Just a chance encounter." Mae who! J. D.'s heart was officially healed. Amazing, the power of lemonade and sugar cookies.

It was fashionably late when he finally left Gramma's house. That was just the medicine that J. D. was lacking. He just needed the right woman to take an interest in him. J. D. was invited over for Sunday dinner. However, he is not sure if J. D. is courting Elizabeth or if Gramma is courting him. I don't think it really matters at this point. He did find out that Liz was seeing a doctor socially, but he ended up joining the Canadian Mounties. So, she has no romantic attachments right now. Liz won't be staying with Gramma permanently. Eventually, she will go back to Montreal and continue working in her father's clinic. His best option was to play it cool and see if anything developed.

Sunday afternoon. J. D. arrived with flowers, a new suit of clothes, and highly shined boots. Liz opened the door and let him in. Gramma was in the kitchen helping Elsie prepare the meal. Liz offered to show J. D. the rest of the house. they walked up the stairs and stepped into her mother's old room. Liz said, "Excuse me for a moment," and walked into an adjacent room. Then she summoned J. D. into the room. Liz was lying on the bed wearing a blue corset. Then Liz said, "J. D., I want you to make love to me. Do you want to?" He started to undress carefully so as not to wrinkle his new suit of clothes. Once undressed, he walked over to the bed and sat down beside her. "J. D., I am thirty-one years old and still a virgin. I can't wait any more. You are an incredibly attractive man, and you are very kind as well. I would very much like you to be my first."

"What about Gramma and Elsie?"

"Well, I am not really into foursomes, but if that is your taste."

Laughing, "No, won't they wonder where we have gone to?"

"Don't worry, they know exactly where we are and what's going on."

"In that case, I would love..." Liz leaned in, started kissing him all over, while dismantling her corset at the same time. Being a nurse, she was well aware of the functionality of her anatomy. After almost an hour had passed, they walked down the stairs together, completely intoxicated by the incredible aromas coming from the kitchen. Gramma spoke up, "Did you show J. D. everything while you were upstairs?"

"Oh yes, everything."

J. D. responded, "It was lovely up there."

"Good. Hopefully, you worked up an appetite. Let's eat, shall we? Elsie! We are waiting on you, dear."

"Sorry, I forgot the gravy." The four of them sat down for a delicious dinner.

"Gramma, after that big meal, I need a little air. May I excuse myself onto the front porch?"

"Oh, please, make yourself at home. My house is yours."

"Thank you." He stood up and made his way to the oak spindle rocking chair on the front porch, sat down, pulled a cigar out of his breast pocket, lit the end, and reflected on how good a day he was having. Then he thought to himself, What exactly is going on here. I know I am a celebrity in certain circles, but this is a little over the top. I don't quite get how befriending me would benefit their circumstance. Maybe Liz is a little star-struck. She said it was her first time. It didn't really seem that way to me. I guess she has read up on the subject quite a bit. Maybe she really was just waiting for the right guy.

Liz walked out onto the porch and sat in the chair next to mine. "J. D., I never thanked you properly for such a wonderful afternoon."

"Yes, you did. In fact, you thanked me twice. I assume I thanked you twice as well."

"Almost three times."

"Okay, I am glad we got all that thanking out of the way. Can I ask you a question?"

"Sure."

"What exactly happened here today? I feel like some kind of royalty right now."

"Gramma is just being her normal self, as a gracious host. As for me, I guess I should tell you that I have a thing for gunfighters. I read the novels as well. You really were my first and a gunfighter too. That just added to the allure. I'm sorry if you feel like I used you. I would never want to compromise our friendship. After what we shared earlier, I hope you would be interested in being more than just friends."

"Liz, I would very much like to see you on a regular basis. Nothing would please me more. I feel I must disclose to you about my past. I have enemies, especially in Texas, but I think I have managed to put that ugliness behind me. There is also an incident in Kansas that could come back to haunt me someday. I don't mind telling you, I like you a lot. You are beautiful, with a wonderful sense of humor, and are very intelligent. I find that very intriguing in a woman. So, you are definitely my type. I guess I'm a little apprehensive because I would never want anyone that I care about to be jeopardized by my violent past."

"J. D., I'm a big girl who can take care of herself. I carry a .44 derringer in my purse for just such an occasion. You needn't worry too much about me. By the way, I am a pretty fair hand with a revolver, and I have a .50 cal. Plains rifle on my mantle at home in Montreal. Dad and I go after Caribou every year."

"Okay, but these enemies of mine, they may try to harm you to get to me. Caribou don't shoot back."

"J. D., can we cross that bridge when we come to it?"

"Okay. By the way. You are not planning to stay here in Toronto permanently, are you?"

"No. I am supposed to return in about six weeks, but I could stay longer and work out of Dad's office here in town had I a good enough reason to stay." She stared right at J. D. while playfully licking her lips.

"Gee, you are as bad as your Gramma."

"Where do you think I learned it from?"

"I should tell you, I am not very well-heeled financially at this point. I have a few thousand sitting in a California bank, and less than a thousand dollars cash right here. I am pulling almost fifty dollars a week as a bouncer. I think that is a decent wage for a guy who got most of his formal education in the Army. I can read every line in the newspaper and run a cash register, too. I'm not dense by any means. You will definitely be the brains in our relationship."

"That's okay, most women like me have need of men well beyond their accounting skills."

"Another question. How long have you been a practicing nurse?"

"Eight years, I went to Nursing School right after I graduated from Finishing School. Dad made me go to Finishing School, or he was never going to let me work for him as a nurse."

"I like your Dad already. You must have a great relationship together if the two of you go Caribou hunting every year."

"Dad is great. He never remarried. I don't think he wanted me to have to deal with an overbearing stepmother. He had tons of opportunity, though."

"I can sympathize with him on that one. The first day I started as a bouncer, women were constantly throwing themselves at me, batting eyelashes, low cut blouses, and wandering hands. That actually has subsided somewhat, thank goodness. The barflies are starting to leave me alone. My last girlfriend left me rather abruptly. She left me a bit of a heartache, but you and Gramma cured me of that the other day. That was the first time since my breakup that I thoroughly enjoyed being in the company of women. I thank you both for that. You do realize that if the strap on your shoe had not broken, we would never have met, or did you break it on purpose?"

"Well… I kind of did. I saw you walk into the saloon when the stage pulled up, and said to myself, that cowboy has got a great ass. But how did you figure that out? I thought I covered my tracks pretty well."

"I wasn't overly suspicious until you seduced me earlier. Then I thought it was a bit too coincidental. I guess when you learned my identity, that must have sealed the deal for you."

"Yes, that put me in infatuation overload. I was so nervous upstairs. I was afraid you might get overwhelmed and leave."

"I was overwhelmed, but I certainly wasn't going anywhere. At least not right away." Gramma and Elsie walked out on the porch and sat down.

"So, are you kids starting to get better acquainted?"

"Yes, Gramma, we are."

"Good. Not for nothing, if I were twenty years younger, I would be catfighting Lizzie over you."

"I would hate to think who would win that battle."

"Speaking of that, you fought in the Mexican-American War, didn't you?"

"Yes, I attained the rank of Major, prior to resigning at the conclusion of the war."

"You didn't want to keep soldiering, from what I read, you had quite a knack for it."

"That's true, the unit I commanded received a commendation. The Army offered me a promotion to Colonel if I stayed in. As a soldier, I was either training for battle, preparing for battle, or fighting a battle somewhere. Don't get me wrong, I enjoyed the glory and attention as much as any man, but I guess I just wanted my life to matter outside the field of battle."

"You sound like you are still on a crusade, maybe as a clergyman or as an attorney."

"No, I never gave much thought at all to religion. Chasing an invisible God is not my thing. I did enjoy my time as a lawman until the showdown with Eli Duncan."

"Soon after that, I headed as far west as I could go to sort things out."

"J. D., I like you a lot. I hope you feel the same way about us."

"I do; I cherish your friendship. Thank you. I really should be heading back. I have the late shift at the saloon tonight."

Liz spoke up, "Can I walk you to your horse?"

"Sure. Good afternoon, Elsie, Gramma. Thank you for a lovely dinner, goodbye." Liz trotted J. D.'s horse out of the barn, handed over the reins, and gave him a very long, passionate kiss. J. D. rode off quickly lest he talk himself into staying for the night. J. D.'s mind began to gather thoughts of being a permanent part of the Thomas family. Liz would make a wonderful wife for some lucky man; why not him? He stopped for a moment and looked back, just barely able to see the very top of Gramma's house. The man could not help being overwhelmed with guilt and depression due to the demons from his past. Selfishly thinking, if I pack up and leave right now, I will shatter a woman's heart and leave her in agony much the same way Mae left me. I can't let the fear of lost love cause me to betray this feeling in my heart. I want Liz to be mine; all mine. I will fight for that privilege.

Chapter 11:
J. D's Dilemma

J. D. arrived back in town. The saloon was busy for a Sunday night. He didn't have to be to work for another couple of hours, but figured on checking with Big Hank just the same. Hank looked relieved to see him walk in. "J. D., you are a welcome sight, my friend. This place has been jumping all day. Can you grab an apron and back me up at the bar?"

"Sure, I'll hop right in there." It was just one of those days when everybody was thirsty for a cold beer. After several hours, the crowd started to thin out, and the two men had a chance to catch their breath. At 11 pm., they pushed the last drunk out the front door and closed the place. Hank grabbed a bottle and two glasses. "Sit down and have a drink with me, you earned it, pal."

"Thanks. You said it was crazy like that all day."

"Pretty much from the time I opened the door, parades of people came in wanting beer, whiskey, champagne, and cigars. We almost sold out of cigars. So, how was dinner with Elizabeth and her family? Did you get the Gramma seal of approval?"

"Yes, and then some. I don't usually get this infatuated with a woman so quickly, but Liz is a pretty amazing woman. No, she is an extremely amazing woman. She is a nurse, beautiful inside and out. Oh yes, she is very intelligent too. If I don't end up married to this woman, I will regret it the rest of my life. My one issue, hangup, problem, dilemma, whatever you want to call it, is my past. I know something in my past is going to upset this wonderful thing I have with Liz. I am just not very lucky when it comes to long and meaningful relationships. Usually, I lost out to richer men in the end. Not so with Mae, she left me for a difference in ideology. That was a new one. I could sort of see that one coming, but I wasn't very wise to what happened. She was great in bed, though. Wow, that woman had a hold on me."

"So, if you care for Liz as much as you say, marry the woman. Go to Montreal and ask her Dad for permission. You have money. You have a job. Just do it."

"Her old man is a big-time physician. He has an office right here in Toronto. Dr. Thomas is his name."

"Yes, I heard of him. Well, I heard of the clinic anyway. They have a good reputation. He hasn't been run out of town on a rail, anyway."

"We have only known each other for a week. It would seem a bit presumptuous on my part. I do like her a lot. I wonder how she feels about kids. I think I definitely need to slow down a bit. I like kids. Mae has two young, almost-grown sons, Andrew and Tommy. I really enjoyed mentoring them. Their Pa got killed in the War. They were both rough around the edges until I started spending time with them. I did make the mistake of teaching them how to shoot. It might have gotten one of them killed. I don't know, with Mae deciding to avenge her son's incarceration, it may have been inevitable. I sure feel lousy about that. Andrew was a good kid. I will miss him."

"Okay, Daddy, how many do you want? I was raised on a farm right outside Baltimore, with a younger brother and two mean older sisters. We used to torment each other something awful. My oldest sister Rosie was a very plain-looking girl, but she made up for it with a lot of character. She would try and dump a bucket of water on my head every chance she got. Pa would get so mad with her for wasting water like that. It didn't really matter. Our well never even came close to running dry. I got her back really good one day. She had a runt pig she raised after the sow stopped letting her suckle. I booby trapped a bag of horse manure right over where she would sit to play with Franklin. I dangled a piece of heavy twine down right beside her ear. It brushed up against her, and she gave it a yank. The next thing, she was covered in horse turds up to her waist. I swear she chased me halfway to Baltimore. Luckily, I could outrun her then. When I got older, I didn't really care for farm life. Crops and livestock just weren't my thing. My Pa was strict about work ethic. Work till sundown. Eat and rest till sunup. All of us kids went to school and got our diplomas. Ma and Pa both saw the benefit of a decent education.

After each of us turned eighteen, we got a twenty-acre plot of land or $200.00 cash in the form of an early inheritance. I took the cash and started a freight company in Baltimore. I sold that business five years later and bought my first Tavern. You know the rest. I have never been married and have no regrets about it. I like a little female companionship on occasion, but that's it for me. Like I said, no regrets. Everybody is different. For some men, the only thing they want is a woman they can wake up next to in the morning. No thanks."

"You are right about one thing; all men are definitely not put together the same way. I learned that bit of information in the Army. I met enlisted men who were smart enough to be really good officers, and I met some officers who couldn't polish their boots worth a damn. The generals, wow, most officers above major were so concerned about their status, they would do anything not to tarnish any part of their reputation. I only met a few decent division commanders. Say nothing of the political appointee commanders; they were clueless on the battlefield. The regular army generals weren't much better. The war between the states is such a catastrophic waste of human life. That's why I decided not to get involved in this one. I may have been able to save a few soldiers from being killed, but I just could not see the point. The arguments that caused the Confederate States to secede were weak at best. The business model of chattel slavery is all but finished. The Founding Fathers should have banned slavery in 1877 and been done with it. Cowards, all of them. The hell with them. Sorry, I didn't mean to rattle on so much."

"No, you have a point, slavery has no place in modern society. End of story."

"Hank, I think we better clean this place up, because I know it won't clean itself up for us. I will start washing mugs and glasses."

"Okay, I will wipe down the bar, tables, and chairs. Then we can both start mopping the floors." It took the two of them, drunk as they were, about an hour to get the place looking presentable again. Afterward, J. D. found his way next door and staggered up to his room to sleep off his sure-to-be doozie of a hangover.

9 am, and the sun shone brightly right into J. D's room. He rolled over and fell out of bed. Last night's binge drinking left him with a terrible case of cottonmouth. His image graced the mirror atop the bureau. "Oh shit, never again." J. D. walked down the hall to the wash basin and stuck his head in and pumped the water on his head. Then he stood up and shook his head violently, turned around, and looked down to discover he was standing in the hallway stark naked. As he walked back to his room, an older couple met him at the end of the stairs.

The woman said, "Good morning, and thank you."

"Any time, madam. Always glad to be of service." J. D. walked back into his room and closed the door behind him. Then he tried to recollect the brief conversation he had just had in the hallway. He started to laugh and fell back on the bed. He thought to himself, "I better get dressed and go get a hot bath, forthwith." So that's exactly what he did. Next stop was a haircut and a shave, then back over to the hotel for breakfast.

J. D. wandered back to the hotel restaurant and sat down at an open table. Then who would come walking out of the kitchen but Gramma's cousin, Elsie. "Good morning, J. D. What would you like for breakfast?"

"Eggs, bacon, coffee, and a question."

"Yes, Gramma and I own this place. I still like to work the breakfast shift a few days a week. It helps to keep up with the books. You made quite an impression yesterday, and this morning. The old couple you bumped into this morning were here an hour ago. You were all they could talk about. Hell, it's probably all over town by now. You must have been really boiled last night. They said you were comatose when they saw you earlier. What happened?"

"Aw, man! I got back to town, and the saloon was just brimming over with patrons. I went in early. Big Hank and I could barely keep up. We closed at 11 pm. Then sat down together and drained a bottle of whiskey. I helped Hank clean up, then staggered to my room. I barely remember that couple this morning."

Laughing, "Well, they sure remember you. I'll get you some coffee." Elsie came back with a full coffee urn and a cup. "I don't mind telling you, Elizabeth is overwhelmed by you. I have to ask. What are your plans here in Toronto and with Elizabeth? She is a grown woman, but I know how cruel men can be."

"Elsie, I assure you, and you can relay this to Gramma Kay as well, I am quite fond of Liz. She is wonderful. Because of that, I had to tell her I have had confrontations with some very bad men in the past. She seemed okay with that. That history has not found its way to Toronto yet. It may never catch up to me. I don't know. It is a concern, though."

"Elizabeth told us that you were very honest and upfront with her. Thank you. That right there tells me you are a keeper."

"Can I ask you a question?"

"Yes."

'What is Dr. Thomas like?"

"Daniel, Dr. Thomas, is a good man and an excellent doctor. I think he will like you. Honestly, the guy she was seeing before was really arrogant. I couldn't stand him. He was handsome. I will concede that, but a bit of an opportunist. He barely graduated from Medical School. I wasn't sorry to see him go. Personally, I put lots of faith in karma. he left to give you the opportunity. This is the happiest I have seen little Lizzie in quite a spell. Thank you for that."

"Elsie, I am very grateful to have the three of you in my life right now. Nothing would please me more than to see this relationship with Liz blossom into something special for both of us."

Smiling, she said, "You are a very eloquent man, J. D. Malone. Your breakfast should be ready." As J. D. polished off his eggs and bacon, he thought, *Now I just have to get past her dad. He sounds like a pretty good guy.*

Elsie came out of the kitchen and told J. D., "Breakfast is on the house. After the morning you already had, you deserve a break. Oh shoot, I almost forgot. We got a letter from Daniel this morning. He is coming here in about six weeks. So, you will get to meet him fairly soon."

"Great, I look forward to it. Thank you for breakfast."

"You're welcome, see you around." J. D. headed back to his room and crashed on the bed for a few hours. His shift didn't start until two in the afternoon. A little over an hour later, a knock on the door woke him up. J. D. shouted, "It's open." Liz walked into the room. "Would you like some company?"

"Sure. Sit down."

"J. D., I thought about what you told me yesterday concerning your rather dangerous past. I have come to the conclusion that it really has no bearing on our relationship now. I mean, yes, you have done things I am sure you would like to forget. By the same token, I don't expect you to become this pious conservative version of yourself just to shield me from the ugliness that people are capable of. I have helped Dad patch multiple bullet holes in men many times. My profession can be very bloody at times. I guess what I am trying to say is, I believe I know what I am getting myself into. I want to be with you right now."

"Liz. I want to be with you, too."

"I don't suppose you want to go riding with me out to Gramma's."

"Can I take a rain check? I'm still trying to get rid of this hangover before I have to go to work."

"Sure. Is there room for me under those covers?"

"Come on, I will make room." J. D. ended up falling back asleep in her arms for another hour. Then J. D. went to work, and Liz headed back to the house. Things were really starting to happen for Josiah in a positive way. For the next month, Liz and J. D. were almost inseparable. Everyone was abuzz over Daniel coming to Toronto for a visit. J. D. was quite nervous still, even though the latest correspondence from Daniel was very warm and encouraging at the prospect of meeting a possible son-in-law. Josiah was not ready to propose yet, but thoughts of marriage were being discussed from time to time.

Chapter 12:
A Taste for Blood

Mae woke up early. She heard something spook the horses. It was moments before the dawn, and looking to be a long day of riding if they were going to get anywhere near Paduka, Kentucky, the supposed location of their next victim. "Wake up, boys. Get your biscuit and bacon. Let's get the lead out. We have some traveling to do today, if we are going to make Paducah by sundown."

Tommy and Luke woke up, tied up their bedrolls, grabbed some breakfast, and jumped in the saddle. The three of them were off at a gallop. The trail to get to Paducah was not easy; they had to avoid picket lines on both sides and one skirmish. They had a birdseye view of the small battle from an adjacent hill. All around them was the stench of dead men and horses. The three of them made the outskirts of town just about sundown. It gave them a chance to get a hot bath and a boiled wash. Something they had not seen since leaving Toronto. Upon finishing her bath, Mae asked the woman who owned the bathhouse exactly where the new Union Headquarters was located.

Mrs. Aubrey informed her that it was the old Courthouse building in the center of town. Afterward, they camped for the night just outside of town on the southern bank of the Tennessee River. Just before Mae began to prepare to get ready to bed down for the night, she called the boys over to discuss how they were going to kidnap the general. "Luke, I want you to enter the courthouse first and find the general's office. I want to get there right at dawn. The guards should be fairly tired at that point. That is, if there are any guards around. I would assume so. It is a headquarters." Luke spoke up, "Ma, if it is a division HQ or higher, then there will definitely be guards posted at every entrance and at the general's outer office."

"What about breakfast?"

"Normally, they would go to the Mess after the guard shift change, usually at around 0800. That might be a good time for me to sneak in. Then I can try to find my way to an empty office with a first-floor window where you can come in. Tommy should keep the horses quiet and out of sight until we have the general. You are planning to kidnap the general, right?"

"Maybe, it might be better to just shoot him in his office."

"Yes, Mae, it might. It just depends on the situation at the time. We still have the element of surprise on our side, which is really a huge advantage for us."

"Okay, boys, let's all get some rest. We need to be fresh and ready in the morning. Good night." Mae didn't sleep much. She was kind of in and out all night, thinking about the life she took earlier. No regrets, though. Kenneth Banks deserved to die. He was a misogynistic waste of a man and only sought to serve himself. The world is full of men like him. Users of others for personal gain. Who teaches them that? How does a young boy suddenly wake up one morning believing that the entire world is theirs for the taking, with no regard for the needs of others? They all need to perish in their own swill. Mae packed up and ate a light breakfast, then woke up Luke and Tommy.

"Rise and shine, boys, daylight is a wasting already. Grab a biscuit and mount up."

Tommy quipped, "No bacon this morning?"

"Sorry, kiddo, we'll get cleaned up and properly fed in West Virginia tomorrow night." The three of them were off and running to downtown Paducah. The town was just beginning to wake up. Luke dismounted once they arrived at the old courthouse. "I will sneak in and find a window on the north side of the building that you can enter through."

Mae said, "We will meet you over there shortly." Luke walked up the steps and entered the building. He was surprised the guards did not stop him. Once inside, the Sgt. of the Guard approached him. "Sgt., is there a privy in here. I had a little too much breakfast."

"Sure, sir, just down the hall to your left. It's just short of the commander's office." Luke trotted down the hall and entered the room. It was perfect. There was a big window with a very low threshold. He popped it open and signaled for Mae to enter. Luke walked through the door and placed himself in a position to cover Mae as she walked casually into the next room. Luke thanked the sergeant, exited the building, and hurried back to where Tommy was staging the horses. Meanwhile, Mae entered the commander's outer office and slowly opened the door to General Mendalbine's office. The man was sitting at his desk.

"Madam, how did you get in here?" Mae revealed her shotgun and pointed it directly at the General's chest. "What is the meaning of this?"

"Sir, you have no regard for the sanctity of human life!" Boom! His dead body slumped forward onto his desk. Mae quickly reloaded, then opened the window leading to a small courtyard outside. Tommy and Luke galloped toward her, and the three of them made a dash to exit the town as fast as their horses would carry them. As they raced east down the main street heading toward the Tennessee River, onlookers were taken aback at the sight of three riders running through town just after 8 am. Some wondered if a bank had just been held up. One old gentleman sitting in a rocking chair in front of the post office commented, "They sure are in a hurry. They weren't loaded down with saddlebags. Probably not a bank robbery." Minutes later, a large group of soldiers on horseback came running in the same direction, hot on their trail.

The Barber spoke up, "Something is definitely afoot, or in the saddle as it were."

The man in the rocker retorted, "Boy, they are definitely after those three for something. You wonder if something happened at the Army HQ in the old courthouse? Look! There are two more soldiers walking into the telegraph office. Looks like I will have to buy Smitty a drink later."

"Smitty, the telegraph operator?"

"Yeah, we go way back to the Mexican-American War."

"You fought in the war?"

"No, we served together in the Quartermaster Corps."

"Oh, right. I forgot. Nonetheless, something is going on for sure."

Shortly, Luke led Mae and Tommy to the southern bank of the Tennessee River, and they ran along the river for a couple of miles before doubling back slightly to lose the Army squad that was sure to be following their fresh tracks. Their ruse worked.

The squad turned back as soon as they reached the riverbank. The Sgt. in charge of the squad told his men, "We're heading back. There's no way of knowing which way they are headed now."

Upon returning to HQ, General Mendalbine's body was being carried out the front entrance with a Union flag draped across him. The Sgt. spoke, "I can't believe we just let them waltz right up and assassinate the General like that. It's going to be hell to pay around here." His men just nodded their heads in somber agreement to what was said.

An officer call was played about ten minutes later. Immediately after being dismissed, the XO, General Marks, left for Washington D. C. to report the incident in person to his superiors. This may not have been a very good decision. It would allow for Mae and the boys to execute their next caper on General Miller, who was currently bivouacked just outside Clarksville, Tennessee. After crossing the Tennessee and Cumberland rivers by ferry, the gang halted in a thick patch of woods to bed down for the night. Mae started a fire, "Ma, there are enemy patrols everywhere around here. I don't think a night fire is a wise thing to do."

"You want hot beans, bacon, and coffee, don't you?"

"Yes, of course, but not at the expense of our freedom." Half a moment later, the three of them were surrounded by a squad of Confederate soldiers. "Ma'am, we haven't eaten much more than crickets and bark tea for the last three days." The Sgt. asked if they could share in a bite of their meal. Mae answered, "Come on in, gentlemen. We have enough for everyone."

"Allow me to introduce myself. I am Sgt. Diggers of the 10th Kentucky Militia. These seven men are all that is left of my platoon."

"I am Willie Mae, and these are my sons, Luke and Tommy. Call me Mae."

"Mae, what are you doing here?"

"Well, we have business in Clarkesville. We are going to kill General Miller. The last word we got, his unit is camped just south of there."

"Wait, you are that vigilante woman, Scattergun Mae Anderson. Ma'am, did you really kill eight Yankee generals?"

"No, General Miller will be number three."

"In that case, Mae, we are going to have to escort you back to our camp, so our commander, Major Stuhill, can talk to you. We are part of a larger force to halt General Miller's advance into Nashville."

"Okay, Sgt. Let's eat and get a move on." The Sgt and his small unit escorted them to the Rebel camp about a quarter mile away.

"Wait here, ma'am. I must report to the Major." Sgt. Diggers walked to the Major's tent and reported what he and his men found on their patrol.

"Sir, I have Mrs. Willie Mae Anderson right outside. She told me that her gang's next target is General Miller."

"Sgt, Mae Anderson is here?"

 "Bring her to me at once."

"By your leave, sir." Mae and the boys were escorted right in.

"Mrs. Anderson, you are a giant thorn in the Union Army's backside right now. They want to hang you. We want to recruit you. Come in, all of you, sit and make yourselves comfortable. The Sgt. informed me that your next target is General Miller. I am afraid I can't let you do that; it may jeopardize my mission. If you were to go after Gen. Miller right now, it would put every enemy unit in Tennessee on full alert. We desperately need the element of surprise in order to stop the General's advance into Nashville. My unit was put together from squads and platoons that were all but wiped out in previous battles. We formed up in Montgomery, AL, especially for this secret mission. I am telling you this in the utmost of confidence. I sincerely hope I can count on you to cooperate with us in this endeavor."

"Well, I once read, the enemy of my enemy is my ally."

"Okay, we will trail you into battle, but if you capture him, you turn him over to me."

"Sure, we will be attempting to assassinate him ourselves during the raid. Actually, our main objective is to neutralize his artillery and destroy his logistics. After that, he's all yours."

"How soon are you scheduled to march out of here?"

"Two days."

"Good, that will give us time to forage the local town for supplies before returning here."

"I would like to offer you a tent for the night and tomorrow night."

"Thank you, Major, we accept."

"Sgt., find these good people a tent right away."

"Sir, yes, sir. Right this way, folks." Mae and the boys finally bedded down for the night. After about fifteen minutes, Mae got up and took a short stroll around the perimeter of the camp. Tommy asked Luke, "Hey, are you awake?"

"Yes, what's up, little brother?"

"Do you think what we are doing is right. Going around killing like this don't feel right somehow."

"Tommy, go ask that Rebel Major if it's right. He will say that it is. What we are doing is collecting on a debt. Pa, John, and Andrew deserve that at least."

"I miss our life back in Missouri. Everything was so much simpler then. We weren't constantly in and out of chaos."

"Look, if you want to know the truth. After fighting in dozens of battles in this war, my justification to keep going was starting to grow thin. Every battle seemed to push my tolerance for bloodshed to the bitter edge. War is war to the final skirmish. Until there is no reason or resolve to go on killing the enemy, the fighting will go on. Just be glad you are not on the front line sweeping artillery shrapnel off your boots."

"Luke, how many men did you kill?"

"Enough to know that they are all waiting for me in Hell. Go to sleep, okay."

"Good night, Luke."

Chapter 13:
Slaughter In the Making

0500 wake-up call. Up before the dawn, break down your tent. Tuck in your bedroll and tie it off on the pack mule. Time to move out. Breakfast, what little of it there was around, got eaten on the move. Mae and the boys fell in the road march between the Ambulance and the Mess Wagon. Hard to tell which smelled worse. The timeline was moved up a day. Miller's Command was thirty miles closer than initially reported. The Major's objective was simple. All he had to do was find a suitable location on the road from Clarksville to Nashville for an ambush.

A narrow passage of road was discovered. It was surrounded by step hills for approximately three-quarters of a mile. The elevation was just enough to conceal dismounted men with rifles. The only hitch was if they could be spotted by General Miller's scouts. Despite Mae being informed to the contrary, Gen. Miller was not a complete idiot. Major Stuhill devised a scheme that would divide Miller's forces. A ruse that would lead the General's Cavalry away from the infantry.

According to Major Stuhill's latest intelligence reports, the Union Army was oblivious to the whereabouts of the Major's Brigade. Given the almost perfect terrain and the element of complete surprise, the day should belong to the Confederacy. Stuhill's scouts spotted Miller's troops almost eight miles north of the ambush site, headed directly for Nashville at a forced march, approximately five miles an hour.

Scouts returned to General Miller. "General, Sir. Corporal Fairson reporting in, sir."

"Yes, what's out there?"

"Sir, we spotted a company of Rebel Cavalry walking their horses five miles ahead of us, crossing the Nashville road at a very leisurely pace. Approximately one hundred and fifty men and horses, sir."

"Colonel Sparks, what do you make of it?"

"It's a gift from the War Gods. An excellent prize for the Corps Commander, sir."

"Yes, I heartily agree. They must be on a reconnaissance mission, being alone this far north. A nice prize indeed. Major Weeks, take your Cavalry, pursue, and destroy the Reb's. Capture anything that is left."

"By your leave, sir." Major Weeks took every horseman under Gen. Miller's command and rode away in a column of twos in pursuit of the Rebel Unit, unaware of the hornet's nest he was about to lead his men into. Shortly, thereafter, the Union Major caught up to his prey only to find approximately two dozen men on horseback brambling at a slow gait.

The Major called out, "Where is the rest of the regiment?" Pistol fire started blazing from the Major's rear.

Major Weeks commanded, "Herringbone, to the rear!" It was too late. The troopers that weren't shot were slashed right off their horses by sabers. Every Union trooper and over half of the horses lay dead or dying. It was a complete slaughter in under three minutes. General Miller would never know what became of his Cavalry.

Major Stuhill's baited surprise attack was a monumental success. Even he was overcome by the one-sided victory. The Major made one last officer's call to ensure the infantry placements in preparation for General Miller's main force, which was at this very moment, rapidly approaching. As soon as the rest of his division fell into rifle range, Stuhill's men would open fire. The Cavalry would remain hidden until after the fourth volley of fire. Then Capt. Williams would advance as part of a coordinated attack with a corresponding infantry bayonet charge.

Stuhill's men lay waiting behind the step hills flanking the Nashville road. The infantry companies have been posted in complete concealment behind the short hills. Strict noise and light discipline by all was imperative to allow the element of surprise to remain intact. In less than an hour, Gen. Miller would be riding up front, leading his men right into the kill zone.

There is always a quiet moment just prior to a skirmish. The new recruits are eager to taste their first war-soaked adrenaline rush. The veterans reflect upon their prayers, the welfare of their families, and themselves. They know all too well that even with the shrewdest of battle strategies, once the fighting begins, confusion is the overriding theme as the two armies test each other's combat efficiency. The Company Commanders receive their final instructions. Major Stuhill firmly expressed to hold all fire until the maximum number of enemy soldiers reached the kill zone.

"Gentlemen, wait for my command to fire, then give them a basted serving of hot lead. Continue for four volleys, then affix bayonets and charge the enemy along with the Cavalry. Good luck men. God save us all this day."

The Major's standard prayer for the men had managed to keep his men alive up to this point. Scouts report Miller's lead element is less than a mile away. Marching in a column of fours. "Alert all companies of the enemy's location and to wait for my command."

Stuhill watched as the enemy came closer and closer through his binoculars. As the first row of Union soldiers passed the end of the firing line, the Major shouted, "Fire!!" A hail of bullets covered the road as almost a third of the enemy in firing range fell wounded or dead where they stood. The remaining volleys were almost as devastating. Panicked Union soldiers tried in vain to engage the Rebels. General Miller, with no cavalry to mount a serious counterattack, was forced to the ground, still attempting to stage some type of retaliatory response. The hellacious fire seemed to come in all directions. After the fourth volley of fire, the hills were saturated with Rebel Infantry charging their position. Simultaneously, mounted Cavalry began attacking at the front and rear of the column. General Miller did the only thing he could after losing well over half his command to musket fire. He ordered the guidon bearer to fly a white flag of surrender.

Every charging Rebel soldier who caught sight of the white flag immediately began to disarm and escort the remaining Union soldiers to a secure area. The battle/ambush on the Nashville road was over in less than fifteen minutes. General Miller was shot twice during the engagement and lay beside his dead horse holding a pressure bandage up to his neck, where blood was still racing out of his body. Major Stuhill approached the dying General and offered a canteen of water. The General struggled to speak coherently but managed to say, "Major, I am as dead as my horse at this point." He choked on the blood running down his windpipe. "Please see that my men receive fair treatment as prisoners of war." The General gasped on his last breath and expired.

Mae, Luke, and Tommy found the Major standing over General Miller. Mae asked, "Is that General Miller sitting there slumped over dead?"

"Yes, Ma'am, He is dead. I'm sorry you missed out on this one. As far as I am concerned. You are free to go your own way again. My mission here is complete. I require nothing else from you. Good luck to you, safe travels."

"Thank you, Major. Maybe we will meet someday under different circumstances."

"I think I would enjoy that very much. I look forward to making your acquaintance again. God's speed in your travels."

The three of them rode north, headed for Clarksville. A quiet little town, but they had three things that Mae was looking for. A bath, a hot meal, and a soft bed. As Mae and the boys rode into town, surprisingly, it was busy for a Sunday morning. Apparently, a Carnival was in town. Lots of things to look at and buy. They had a slight difficulty finding rooms for the night. The first two hotels they tried were full. Success was finally achieved at the Clarksville Inn. The boys walked over to the Barber shop for a cut and shave. The establishment was open on Sunday, maybe due to the festivities. Luke and Tommy walked in the door and overheard one of the local town folk speaking, "Yup, Scattergun Mae got another one. This one right between the eyes. She is a real brush cutter with that shotgun of hers. I hope I never see the business end of that thing." Luke spoke up. "Not much chance of that in this town. There is no military post here. I heard she only likes to kill generals."

The barber piped in, "Yeah, she is crazy for the generals. I wonder if General Wise has any idea who she is?"

The old man quipped, "Wasn't Gen. Wise with her at Fort Hays?"

"I don't know. What's your pleasure, sir?"

"Shave and haircut, please."

"Coming right up." The old man continued, "I thought I saw the general in town yesterday. I'm sure he would be very interested to know where she is right now. I would give anything to see that meeting take place. I don't think it would end well for Gen. Wise."

Luke commented, "I heard, mind you, I don't know how good the information is, but I did hear that Scattergun Mae and her associates got caught by a brigade of rebel soldiers."

The barber added while finishing up Luke's shave, "I guess that is the end of it." Tommy was next in the chair for a haircut. The old man pointed outside to a horse tied up across the street in a saloon decorated with a two-star blanket. "That's the General's horse right there."

Luke perked up, "Well, what do you know about that. Somebody ought to let him know that Scattergun Mae is in the custody of The Confederacy right now." The old man scooted out the door and across the street to inform the general of the rumor he had just been a party to. General Wise laid his shot glass down on the bar and laughed, "No, sir, the latest information we have puts Mae Anderson somewhere back in Canada, probably Toronto. We would know if she and her so-called gang were anywhere around here."

Everyone went back to having their drinks. About ten minutes later, a woman armed with a shotgun and two freshly groomed gentlemen walk into the saloon. General Wise almost did a double-take. He gulped down the half-full shot of whiskey he was sipping and said, "Scattergun Mae, what the hell are you doing in Tennessee?"

She answered, "Killing you, General Wise!"

Then she emptied both barrels into the General's chest. "Good day to you, gentlemen." Mae, Luke, and Tommy turned and walked toward the door. A single shot rang out. Mae grabbed her right upper hip and leaned over, catching the doorway. Luke and Tommy immediately fired at the soldier who shot at Mae. Then they waved their pistols across the small group of men left at the bar.

"Any more heroes in the room?" Tommy helped Mae onto her horse, and the three of them rode out of town as fast as Mae could gallop in her condition. After doubling back at the crossroads about five miles out of Clarksville, Luke checked Mae's wound. "Good, the bullet went straight through. All we need to do is stop the bleeding, and you should be ok, but we have got to take care of this soon. You probably lost a good bit of blood. Let's head for that tree line and find some good concealment while I doctor up Ma here."

They found a very secluded opening in the heavy brush that was not visible from the meadow they had just crossed. Luke was able to stop the bleeding once they touched the black powder off to cauterize the wound, but Mae fainted. "Don't worry, Tommy, we need to let her sleep now. You get some rest too. I am going to take the horses up to the crossroads just the other side of the meadow. With any luck, any posse sent out from Clarksville will follow those tracks due east. Well, it looks like we are back on cold rations for the next few days. Keep an eye on Ma and keep her warm while I'm gone."

Luke returned an hour and a half later to find Ma and Tommy fast asleep. Ma's wounds looked ok for now. Later, they would have to make a poultice or find some honey to keep down any infection.

Chapter 14:
A Storm in Washington D. C.

General Marks arrived in Washington D. C. to request an audience with Secretary of War William Feddelson. He promptly tied his horse and proceeded into the War Department located on Pennsylvania Avenue. To his delight, the General was escorted into Secretary Feddelson's outer office and instructed to wait while the Captain announced his arrival.

The Captain returned and held the door open as General Marks reported to Sec. Feddelson.

"General, I have never had the pleasure of meeting you in person. What news from the front?"

"Sir, General Mendalbine was murdered a week ago by Scattergun Mae Anderson and her gang. She also killed General Banks over three months earlier. I felt that I should report to you in person and fill you in on just exactly how he died, sir." Feddelson sat back in his desk chair in disbelief, hearing for the first time that a woman killed two commanding generals in broad daylight.

"General, are you telling me that this 'Scattergun Mae Anderson' just stood up during a General Court Martial, kidnapped Gen. Banks, and shot him minutes later?"

"Yes, sir. That's pretty much what happened. One of her gang members was killed during the escape. I think that was probably what pushed her over the edge." The Captain brought Sec. Feddelson an urgent telegram. He read the telegram informing him that Adjutant General Wise had been murdered in Clarksville, Tennessee, at the hands of 'Scattergun Mae Anderson.' Sec. Feddelson bellowed, "Captain Banton, I want my entire senior staff to report to me in this office in five minutes! And Captain, I don't mean six minutes either!"

Approximately five minutes later, Generals' Monty Patricks, Elvin Nord, Steven Slaggert, and Wallace Pritner walked into the office one by one. Sec. Feddelson welcomed the generals and offered them chairs surrounding his conference table. "Gentlemen, I just have one simple question. Whose idea was it not to tell the Secretary of War that one of his generals was found on a prairie stripped naked and shot in the chest with a double-barreled shotgun by a grieving widow from Missouri? Okay, I am waiting patiently." One hand was raised. Sarcastically, Sec. Feddelson quipped, "Steven, would you like to elaborate on the reason why I was not in possession of this bit of information right away. Please, do tell."

"Sir, we, or I should say my staff and I, felt it necessary to eliminate the possibility of the press getting a hold of the story. That is why Gen. Nord and I tried to put a lid on the situation."

"Gentlemen, need I remind you that the press always finds out about everything eventually. Thank God I haven't heard from the president on this issue yet. I give it twenty-four hours before I get an invitation to the white house and get my ass handed back to me on one of the first lady's silver-plated platters she is always raving on about. Oh, and one more question. Who put Kenneth Banks in full command of Fort Hays, superseding Sean Foster?"

Steven raised his hand again. Then he commented, "I owed the man a big favor going back to the Academy. I didn't think it would hurt anything putting him in charge for a week or two."

Feddelson retorted, "More like two months! Steve, you are officially relieved. Clean out your office immediately. I will have a new assignment for you shortly. I'm sorry, but in our business, that kind of favoritism gets people killed. Steven, you are dismissed.

Next question, who was the inside man at Fort Hays? There is no way you can tell me that a widow and two sons pulled off that big of a caper by themselves. Who was it? General Pritner spoke up, "Major J. D. Malone, sir."

"Josiah had a hand in this, the Irish Dandy, really!"

"Sir, we think that Josiah broke away from the gang soon after the Banks killing."

"To hell with the press, let them print what they want. I want a bounty of $5000 put on Mae Anderson, dead or alive. I want $1000 bounties for any surviving gang members."

Pritner retorted, "Sir, I think we may need Josiah's help in apprehending Mae Anderson. We should offer him a pardon for his part in the kidnapping."

"I want J. D.'s mug right next to Mae's on a wanted poster posted in every brothel, sheriff's office, and saloon in this country. Tell him if he doesn't help us put Mae Anderson into custody, he will die doing hard labor in a U.S. Federal prison. Also, remind him he can easily be extradited from Canada now that the laws have been changed."

"Yes, sir, I will hand-pick a team to recruit Josiah, apprehend Mae Anderson, and track down her gang. I don't honestly know how long this mission will take."

"Just find her. We don't even know how many men she may have killed up to this point. The body count may be a lot higher than we think. Men, I probably don't have to tell you how gargantuanly displeased I am right now. This is an embarrassment that the Army could have done without. I don't even want to think of what the Confederate press is going to write when they get ahold of Mrs. Anderson's story. Well, that is all for today, men. Dismissed."

As soon as Gen. Pritner arrived back at his office, he requested Major Bartholamew McKay report to him as soon as possible. Two hours later, the Major reported as ordered.

"Bart, good to see you again. I have a new assignment for you. This mission is classified, so no press. I need you to find 'Scattergun Mae Anderson' along with her gang and arrest them. She and two of her sons are going around killing Union Generals. It needs to be done as quickly as possible. Obviously, I would like them alive so they can stand trial. We need to make an example of her and discourage this type of vigilante behavior going forward at this point. If you can believe it, Major J. D. Malone was riding with her in the beginning. He definitely had a hand in the successful kidnapping and execution of General Kenneth Banks. Sec. Feddelson wants Josiah to work with us. We are offering him a full pardon if he helps in the apprehension of the 'Anderson Gang.' Our latest intel has him living in Toronto, Canada. You can start there. Bart, do not underestimate this woman. She is as dangerous as they come. We know of three victims she executed at close range."

"Wally, I would like to get eight men from line companies temporarily reassigned to me during this mission, which I think I will name 'Operation Vigilante Widow.' I can give the names to your aide on my way out."

"Are these men capable of doing the job?"

"Very, they are all former lawmen and/ or bounty hunters. Just don't put them near a saloon or a brothel. You may have trouble coaxing them out of there."

"Good, I will leave you to the job of disciplining these men as you see fit. There is a $5000 bonus if Mae Anderson is brought in alive."

"I will do my best to see that that happens, but if Mae and her gang are as tough as you say, that may not be an easy task."

"Hopefully, you will have Josiah with you. If anyone can convince this woman to come in peacefully, it would be him."

"Wally, have the men sent to my home in Baltimore after they arrive here."

"Will do, Bart. You take care of yourself." The two men embraced, then Bart retreated to the outer office and relayed his special instructions on how to contact the men he requested for the mission. Major McKay returned to his home in Baltimore and waited for his band of ruthless thugs to arrive. Every one of them was a former lawman, but legalism is not necessarily what this group is about. They are more about collecting bounties. Almost a week later, the men started to show up one by one. As the last man arrived from Indiana, Mackay's squad of enforcers was ready to make the journey to Toronto and recruit Josiah Malone for their mission.

Chapter 15:
Josiah and Daniel Meet

Dr. Daniel Thomas arrived on the noon stage after a very rough ride from Montreal. He was greeted by Josiah, Liz, and Elsie. Gramma was waiting back at the house. Gramma stayed home to add all the finishing touches to the reunion celebration. Daniel had not been back to see his Mama in over two years. He mostly relied upon Elizabeth to keep tabs on her. As the buggy pulled up to the front steps, Daniel and the ladies made their way into the house. Josiah stowed the buggy and bedded down the mare. Then he joined the others, just getting ready to sit down for dinner.

Daniel spoke up, "So, Josiah, I understand that you have managed to steal away my daughter's heart. I should ask what exactly your intentions are toward Elizabeth at this point?"

"Sir, I would very much like to ask for your daughter's hand in marriage. Then J. D. produced a ring from his front jacket pocket."

"Well, son, don't hand it to me. Give it to Elizabeth with my blessing."

"Yes, thank you." Josiah knelt down beside Liz and said, "Elizabeth Banks, I love you with all my heart. I ask you this day in front of your family to marry me?" He handed her the ring. She placed it on her finger and shouted, "Yes!" Then she kissed Josiah, and everyone expressed tears of joy at this jubilant moment. Then they dug into the lemon pepper chicken and all the fixings to go with it. After completely gorging themselves and the dishes had been washed, Daniel and Josiah retired to the front porch for a glass of whiskey and a cigar. "Josiah, I do have one concern, though. This General Banks thing. It has been getting lots of press lately. Are you worried about being extradited back to Oklahoma?"

"Yes, I am. I expected to see wanted posters months ago, but so far, none. From what I have been able to find out, the incident was so embarrassing to the War Department that they are reluctant to prosecute."

"Son, I hope that holds up for you." Daniel heard intense conversation and laughter coming from the parlor inside. "What do you think the girls are up to in there?"

"I am sure that it has to do with the wedding plans."

"Had you and Elizabeth discussed marriage prior to today?"

"Yes, we did. I was just waiting to get your blessing."

"Getting back to that Fort Hays thing, what exactly happened? The newspapers said that this General Banks was in the middle of a court martial, then you, Mae Anderson, and two of her sons basically walked out the front door with the General and her other son, who was formerly in custody."

"Yes, the plan was to release Banks at our staging area, approximately five miles north of the fort. Then we would mount our horses and haul ass to Canada. That plan changed when Mae's son Andrew was shot and killed while escaping. Something snapped in her. Mae executed Gen. Banks, which in her mind avenged Andrew's death. Now it is apparent she has declared some sort of private war of her own against tactically inferior Union Generals."

"I can't believe the U.S. Army is letting this happen."

"Based on my experience as a former officer, I am a little surprised at their response to this, but I am not completely shocked at them trying to bury the incident. I read a news story claiming that Gen. Banks committed suicide. Mae was actually pissed off that the Army covered it up. She wanted someone held accountable for the death of her family members. That's when we parted ways about five months ago. I tried my best to talk her out of any further killing, but she had already convinced herself that what she was doing eased the suffering of widows like her everywhere. Mae Anderson is one of the most passionate and stubborn women I have ever known."

"You loved her, didn't you?"

"Yes, at one point, I had very strong feelings for her. That all ended when they rode out early one morning and left me a goodbye letter. She asked me not to follow her. I burned the letter almost immediately. I am certainly better off without Mae. Now I can concentrate on building a beautiful, meaningful life with Liz. I lost a former wife several years ago. Mae helped me overcome that loss, and for that I will always be eternally grateful, but her vengeful ideology is something I cannot share with her. I choose Liz as my life partner from this moment forward."

"Well-spoken sir. " Daniel looked down at his glass and realized it was empty. "It's time for another round." He scrambled back to the parlor and grabbed the whiskey decanter, then proceeded back to the porch. "Another drink son?"

"Yes, thank you, sir. Now I have a question. Will Liz and I live here or in Montreal after we are married? Liz talked about working out of your Toronto office. Is that a real possibility?"

"Sure, that's the other reason I am here. I like to keep tabs on the Toronto office as well. Normally, I visit once a year, but last year I had two long-time staffers pass away on me. I was so shorthanded, I could not get away. This year, I am fully staffed again. As for where you choose to live, that is completely up to y'all."

The two men picked up their glasses and walked into the parlor, where a very lively conversation about wedding dress alterations was underway. Josiah spoke up, "I guess I will have to invest in another suit for the wedding. By the way, we haven't set a date yet." The women giggled and laughed. Gramma said, "We took the liberty of setting the date three months from now. That should give us time to get all the details arranged. All you men have to do is show up in your Sunday best formal wear. Yes, Josiah, you will definitely need to purchase a new suit of clothes. New boots, a collared shirt, and a tie as well. Just leave everything to us girls, and it will be fine."

"Daniel, do you think we can handle our end of this shindig?"

"Most definitely."

Josiah spoke again, "About the money to pay for the wedding, I would like to contribute some or possibly all that is required to cover the expenses."

"That is a nice gesture on your part, but traditionally it falls upon me as father of the bride to pay all the expenses."

"Are you sure? I have over three thousand dollars of expendable income in the bank right now."

"Yes, I insist on paying for everything. I have been waiting a long time for this." Josiah was quietly elated with the prospect of being married to Liz. They both were convinced that true, passionate, romantic, enduring love had found them. Now it was just waiting for the blessed day to come.

After all the hugs, kisses, and well-wishes were complete, it was time for Josiah to go to work. He was now splitting time between bouncing and bartending. Of course, nobody was dumb enough to challenge him to a gunfight. Josiah was also an accomplished pugilist. Several men have tried to slip a sucker punch at him, but they all always end up lying on their backsides in very short order. When Mr. Malone is working, no one gets cheeky or brave about anything. Most of the regular patrons were very appreciative of the calming atmosphere that Big Hank has been able to create. The place is packed almost every night. There were three other saloons within a mile of Hank's place, but those establishments relied on the customers to bounce any undesirable patrons. Just that fact alone made "The Broken Rein" very popular with the local yokels. Josiah locked the door at the close of business.

"J. D., come sit down and have a drink. There's something I would like to talk to you about."

"What's up, boss?"

"Sir, I can't tell you how big an impact you have had on this place. Bar fights are down to a nil, and we never have shootings anymore. I have only seen you draw your gun twice since you came to work for me. Long story short. I would like to bring you on as a junior partner. Twenty percent of this place would be yours if you want it.

Additionally, I have had plans to upgrade the interior of this place and add a performance stage for live entertainment. I feel the time is right to move forward. Is that something you would be interested in?"

"Well, Hank, I am not sure where Liz and I are going to live once we get married in a few months. If we stay in Toronto, like I think we will, then definitely yes. I hope this includes hiring more workers."

"Yes, I think we will need at least four more people to run this place correctly and show a consistent profit."

"Okay, Hank, I just need to talk to Liz and tell her I would like to stay here in Toronto. I am pretty confident she will go for it, though. She told me she would move here from Montreal if a good enough reason were to arise." Josiah headed out of town the next morning to see if Liz would be interested in staying in Toronto permanently. He arrived just in time for breakfast. As he walked in the door, Gramma announced, "Elsie, Josiah is here. Add another place setting at the table." Josiah kissed Gramma on the cheek, then she proceeded to pinch him on his backside. Gramma, you are awful.

"Yeah, yeah, but if Liz ever cuts you off, I will come scratching on your bedroom door."

"Speaking of Liz, where is she? I need to speak to her." Liz came walking down the stairs. "I am right here, sweetheart. Okay, gramma, get your hands off my man's behind, and go finish preparing breakfast. Remember, I saw him first."

"I'm going, I'm going."

"Honey, I don't mind the teasing by Gramma. In fact, it's kind of flattering."

"What are you saying, you want to poke my grandmother?"

"Oh God no, can we change the subject?" They leaned in for a long, wet kiss.

"Yes, let's do that. Why did you come to see me so early?"

"Well, I had a very interesting conversation with Hank after work last night. Hank asked me if I wanted to be a junior partner with twenty percent ownership of the saloon. If we are going to live in Toronto permanently, I want to do it. Would you consider moving to Toronto?"

That's funny, because I was just going to ask you if you would consider living in this house together so we can assist Gramma later on, as she starts to slow down considerably."

"Yes, nothing would please me more than to live here and become a permanent part of your family. Wow, I guess it is settled then. I will tell Hank later on this afternoon that I want to become part-owner of the saloon."

"Congratulations, honey, I am very happy for you." Daniel came walking down the stairs. "Congratulations for what?"

"I am about to become part-owner of the 'Broken Rein Saloon.'"

"Excellent, that is great news." Elsie announced, "Come and get it." Everyone scurried to the table and sat down for breakfast. Liz announced their plans to stay in Toronto and move in with Gramma permanently after the wedding. It was starting off to be a very good day all around. After breakfast, Josiah returned to the saloon to tell Hank the good news.

"J. D., I am very pleased that you decided to accept my offer. Let's lock up real quick and head over to the bank. I have to get your name added to some documents there. Then we have to visit City Hall for more paperwork. After that, it is done, I will have your name added to the Marquee out front as soon as I can. I would like you to take over as inventory manager. In other words, I want you to start ordering the booze and cigars right away."

"Sure, right away."

Chapter 16:
Mae's Trip to D. C.

"Ma, explain to me again why we have to kill General Slaggert."

"I told you, he is the one that put Banks in charge of Fort Hays. If any man has it coming, it would be him for making such a monumental bonehead move like that." Luke interjected, "Ma, I agree this man made a very poor decision, but executing him?"

"Luke, it comes down to accountability."

"I understand, but when all of this is over, the three of us could face a very violent death."

"Yes, son, you are right about that." Tommy asked, "Ma, how do you feel? Do you think you can ride with that bullet hole in you?"

"If Luke's stitches hold up, I should be ready to ride tomorrow morning. I am still sore around there. Hand me down that bottle of whiskey. That should put me to sleep quickly. Tomorrow morning, we will head for Washington D. C. and rendezvous with Slaggert. Luke, how long should it take to get there on horseback?"

"I figure two weeks at least, with you still healing up. Any faster and you are bound to pull out those stitches. Plus, we are bound to be a hot commodity by now. We can't afford to be seen during the day. Any business we need to conduct will have to be conducted at dusk or later. Do we have enough cold rations for the trip to D. C.?"

"We have plenty of cold rations. We need some fresh water, though. We are down to half a keg."

"We should be fine until we hit another good-sized town. We are very fortunate not to have seen a wanted poster with our mugs on it. I would have bet anything there would be paper on us by now, even if it's just a general description. We should scout the Sheriff's office in the next town we come to. We all need a hot bath desperately. Personally, I am getting sick of bathing in cold streams every time we stop for the night. Soap would be nice too."

"What's the matter, boy? Are you starting to itch down there?"

"As a matter of fact, yes! That and a few other things I would like to take care of. The two of you aren't exactly the company I had expected to keep every night of this journey since my escape from Fort Hays."

"Oh, I did notice that you spent many nights at Madame Estelle's establishment in Toronto. Maybe that's where that itch you have down under came from?"

"Okay, Ma, that's my cue. I am going to bed."

Tommy asked, "What kind of itch have you got?"

"Don't worry about it, kid, I will explain it to you at the next town. Good night."

The next morning was day one of their trek to the nation's capital, where they expected to find their next victim. The journey would require crossing the Southern Appalachian mountains unless they took a detour through Atlanta, but that would put them in close proximity of a ghastly group of troops, both northern and southern. Following the Virginia-Pennsylvania border would be the best safest route, allowing the best odds of not being detected by scouts or picket lines.

Stoneville, TN, was the next sleepy little town they came to after a long day in the saddle. The three of them desperately wanted clean sheets to rest on. However, Luke was interested in pursuing a slightly more physical distraction before actually going to bed. Luke led Ma and Tommy into town right after sunset. The first stop was a saloon to get a drink and rest Ma's saddle sores. The bullet wound was definitely starting to take a toll on Mae's ability to stay in the saddle. They ordered a bottle and sat down. This time, Luke requested three glasses. Tommy would get his first taste of hard liquor.

Luke bellowed, "Drink up, kid, you are going to get a lesson in manhood tonight. no man should die a virgin."

"I am not a virgin! I kissed Wilma Parsons right on the mouth, and she kissed me back."

"Brother, that's not enough to qualify you as a non-virgin. Come on upstairs with me. One of the girls will explain everything to you. Ma, I will be back in an hour or so. Tommy will probably be back much sooner."

"Okay, boys, go and get it over with. I may head over to the bathhouse to get cleaned up. while you are busy."

"Sure, Ma, we will see you later." Tommy followed Luke upstairs for his first completely intimate experience with a woman. Luke procured the services of Francine for Tommy. Then she escorted him into a private room.

"Tommy, is it okay if I call you Tom?"

"Yes. Francine, you are the prettiest girl I have ever seen."

"Tom, have you ever seen a real, completely naked woman before?"

"No, never."

"You can call me Fran, everyone else does." She began to undress for him. Tommy became extremely excited. It was obvious by his enormous erection. He leaned forward on the bed and touched Fran's breasts. She laid on the bed beside him and spread her legs. "Tom, this is what the fuss is all about. Go ahead, you can touch it, but it's better when you put your cock in it." Fran proceeded to lay Tom back on the bed and crawl on top of him.

He whispered loudly, "Oh yes! Yes! Faster! Please Faster!"

Then he let out a huge gasp and sighed. Fran leaned over and kissed Tom on the lips, and almost immediately, Tom's erection was back again. Fran began to ride him again. This time it took a bit longer. "Tom, do me a favor, don't tell anyone I did you twice. I am not supposed to do that, but I always like to take special care of my first timers. By the way, you look familiar. Did you grow up around here?"

"No, I was born in Missouri." Then she recognized him. "You are Tommy Anderson! Is your Ma here? Don't worry, I grew up in Alabama. I have no sympathy for the Union if that's what you're worried about. You are not my first customer with his picture on a wanted poster."

"You met Luke. Ma should still be down at the bar finishing her drink. I think she is starting to drink too much. The bullet wound she sustained from the last shootout has taken a bit of a toll on her."

"You better get out of here. If the Sheriff sees you guys, he will try and arrest you for sure."

"We only come to town at night, so we don't get recognized."

"Look, you better be careful. The bounty on Mae and the rest of your gang together is $8000. The government wants you real bad."

"We will be riding out early tomorrow morning. I think you are right, I should be moving on. Thank you for everything."

"You be careful, honey." Fran gave him very passionate goodbye kiss that would perplex Tommy's dreams for many nights to come. He walked out the door and down the stairs to join Ma again at the bar. "Come on Tommy, Luke will definitely be a while. I want a bath and to get my clothes washed."

"Sure, Ma. We got to be careful. My temporary girlfriend recognized me and said there's a huge bounty on us."

"I'm sure she isn't the only one who knows who we are. I had several men look me over in that saloon we were in." Ma and Tommy walked into the bathhouse down the street. The proprietor welcomed them by name and asked if they wanted a bath and boiled wash. Mae answered, "Yes, for both of us, thank you." The owner, Artie Smith, reassured them they were safe in this town. Apparently, Union Cavalry came through the area about a month ago, confiscated food and supplies, and burned several farm houses and barns to the ground. The town shared a genuine distaste for anything to do with the Union at that point. "I assure you, Mrs. Anderson, that your stay in Stoneville will be safe and secure."

"That's good to know, but just in case someone has other ideas, I will be holding you personally responsible for our safe conduct while we rest and recuperate here."

Nervously, he retorted, "Yes, ma'am, we will do our very best to see that you are not molested in any way." Artie exited the tub room with all the dirty clothes. Luke walked in and joined Ma and Tommy in a hot bath. "So, Tommy, Francine said you made quite an impression on her. We may die bloody tomorrow morning, but at least you will have had the pleasures of complete female companionship at least once in your life."

Tommy spoke up, "Actually, it was twice, but she told me not to tell anyone."

"It's okay, man, your secret is safe with me."

Mae interrupted, "I am happy for both of you, but can we please change the subject. I would rather not talk about your sexual exploits while I am laying naked in a bathtub if you don't mind." In unison, "Sorry, Ma."

Chapter 17:
Mackay's On a Mission

Major Mackay and his squad of shootists were about a day out of Toronto in Buffalo, New York. Bart decided he wanted his men clean and respectable for their arrival the following day. This was a mistake because every member of his squad proceeded to get roaring drunk at the first saloon they came to. Subsequently, one of his men ended up getting in a barfight with a local lumberjack and tossed in the city jail. Bart had to pay a ten-dollar fine to get the man released. The rest of his men slept off their bender in a hay loft at one of the livery stables. This little fiasco cost the Major another delay in arriving at their destination.

Upon entering the city limits of Toronto, Bart escorted his men to a bathhouse and chaperoned them to the nearest hotel. He approached the concierge and requested 4 rooms for the night. Bart asked, "Sir, where would I find J. D. Malone? I understand he resides here now."

"You can find him at the 'Broken Rein Saloon' four blocks north of here. They are open until 11 pm. You can't miss the place."

"Thank you."

Mackay mustered up his squad, "You men stay here. I will go and meet J. D. by myself. Do not leave this hotel. It is 8:45 pm now. If I do not return by midnight, come looking for me, but not until then. Dismissed."

Bart mounted up and rode down the street. He tied up his horse and walked into the saloon. He spied J. D. working behind the bar. Josiah recognized him right off and came out from behind the bar and shook hands with his old friend. "Bart, it is great to see you, but I have a bad feeling this is not a social call."

"J. D., I need to talk with you privately right now."

"Okay, let me tell my partner, and we can go to my hotel room and talk." He led Bart to his room next door, and Josiah poured both of them a drink. "I can guess why you are here. It's about Fort Hays, isn't it?"

"I am afraid so. Right now, there is a $1000 reward for your capture, dead or alive, in the U.S. I have a squad of men with me, and we have been instructed by the Secretary of War to bring you back to Washington, D.C., dead or alive. However, the War Department is willing to grant you a full pardon for the kidnapping and murder of General Banks if you join my outfit and help me capture Mae Anderson and her two sons. Make no mistake, you will be brought back to the U.S. one way or the other. We can have you extradited from Canada very easily."

"Look, I am getting married in a couple weeks. I can't leave. I have a new life up here. I really thought I could get away from all that."

"J. D., what happened at the court-martial?"

"It was a disaster. We were only supposed to borrow General Banks long enough to get Luke Anderson out of Fort Hays. During the escape, one of the younger brothers, Andrew, took a mini ball in the back. He died a minute or two later. At that point, Mae snapped. Then she blew the miserable bastard away. At that point, she lost her husband and two sons. We all headed up here. I begged her to let it go and not pursue any more generals, but it didn't take. That was when we parted ways."

Bart remarked, "I kind of figured that was how it went down. By the way, you don't have to worry about General Wise coming after you for that bump on the head you gave him. Mae shot him as well. Hey! What's this about you getting married?"

"Yes, I am supposed to in a few weeks, but it looks like that will be on hold. I don't suppose you could say you didn't find me."

"I can't do that even if I wanted to. If I don't report back to my men by midnight, they will be coming after you. I put together a real nasty group of men to go after you and the 'Anderson Gang.' I figured I would need that sort of ruthlessness to go after her. At this point, she is nothing but a stone-cold assassin."

"Yeah, I know. She is, like you said, ruthless when it comes right down to it. I can probably help you find her, but she is not going to be happy to see me working with you. Any idea where she is now?"

"No, not a clue. What about you?"

J. D. commented, "She killed General Wise. I don't think she was targeting him from the beginning."

"Well, I think you may be right about that. My investigation into the Wise assassination leads me to believe it may have been a crazy coincidence that they ran into each other. The barber in Clarksville thought that the Andersons were there just to get cleaned up and resupplied. They seemed genuinely surprised to find out the General was there."

"Bart, I think her next target will be someone higher up in Banks' chain of command. She already killed General Miller, right?"

"No, he died in an ambush, losing his entire command at the same time."

"Christ, these commanders really are idiots. Okay, who is next in Miller's chain of command?"

"General Bryan out of Ohio."

J. D. thought for a minute. "No, Mae would have very little chance of knowing about Bryan. She would definitely go after one of Wise's commanders. I heard some scuttlebutt back at Fort Hays that when Gen. Banks first arrived, he was given temporary command by some friend of his in the War Department. Sean Foster was really pissed off about it. She is definitely headed to Washington D.C. We have to get there before she does. We will need to secure passage by train."

"J. D., I guess this means you agree to the terms of the pardon."

"Yes, I will help you arrest Mae and her sons in exchange for complete exoneration of my role in the incident at Fort Hays. When do we need to leave?"

"As early as possible tomorrow morning."

"Okay. I will be waiting for you here in the morning, ready to mount up." After Bart left, Josiah jumped on his horse and raced to the house. It was after dark when he arrived, and he startled Liz and Daniel in the parlor.

J. D. announced, "I got really bad news. That problem that I thought was behind me in Kansas just sprang up and bit me on the ass like a timber rattler. I have to go back to the States and help hunt down a fugitive gang wanted by the U.S. War Department." J. D. gave full disclosure of everything, even the part about the ongoing affair with Mae Anderson. Liz began to cry a bit. Daniel spoke, "How long will you be gone?"

"I am not sure, a month maybe more. They may need my testimony at trial, if it comes to that."

Liz asked, "They are offering you a full pardon for everything you did in Kansas, right?"

"Yes, they are. I prayed that this day would never come. I have no choice but to cooperate with them." Daniel retorted, "Josiah, I long suspected that there would be some quid pro quo from your past at some point. You have been given a way out of this mess. You should take it and move on with your life. This may tarnish your reputation a bit, but life is not always fair that way."

Liz followed, "Darling, I want to be the wife of Josiah Malone, local businessman and father of my soon-to-be-conceived children. I care little at all for the shootist and war hero 'Irish J. D. Malone.' Come back to me and be my loving husband." Tears encapsulated Josiah's eyes as he caressed and kissed his future bride.

Daniel asked, "When are you leaving?"

"Early tomorrow morning. Folks, I have to head back to town and let Big Hank know what is going on." He kissed Liz once more, said all his goodbyes, and headed back to town.

Chapter 18:
Chasing Down a Friend

Seven ruthless men and one despondent fugitive boarded a train to Washington D. C. with Major Mackay. The ride was long, and it gave J. D. much time to think back on the entire ordeal and the probable outcome that would surely transpire in a matter of weeks. Mackay has formulated a plan to trap his quarry using J. D. as bait.

"I have to tell you, Bart, I am not crazy about deceiving Mae into thinking I want to join the gang again. I will have to consummate my relationship with her again, and I have a beautiful young fiancée waiting for me in Toronto."

"I know it won't be easy reestablishing that relationship, but remember she was the one who left you, right?"

"Yes, you are right about that. She did break it off with me. And she will likely be very happy to see me again."

"J. D., my spies in Virginia tell me that Mae and her boys are held up in Roanoke. Apparently, she is treated like royalty in every southern town they stop in. We will be in D.C. tomorrow afternoon. then it's three days to Roanoke on horseback."

"Bart, I have been taking this promise of a pardon on faith. I am not just being set up by the war department, am I?"

"I asked General Pritner that same question. I have known Wally Pritner for a long time. I have no reason to think that this offer isn't legitimate. All you did was help a friend's family member out of a really bad situation. To be frank, this entire Anderson Gang mess is Gen. Banks' fault. Honestly, if Mae Anderson had listened to you and not pursued any more generals after Fort Hays, the entire matter would have been swept under the rug, and Bank's cause of death would have been officially listed as a suicide. End of story. Nobody wanted Luke Anderson to be court martialed. He was a hero for pity's sake."

"You got that right. Luke got the raw end of the stick. I hate it when the politics of war comes down to nothing but saving face. Subordinates get sacrificed, and commanders get promotions and commendations. It's really a dirty business."

"When I get to D.C., how do I get travel money to get me to Roanoke?"

"Don't worry, I will get you set up on the first day we arrive in D.C. Let's get some shuteye while we can. You need to catch up with Mae as soon as you can. Don't try to contact me until you have confirmed Mae's next victim. In fact, don't contact me at all until you get back to D.C. I do not want anything to make Mae suspect you are not absolutely on the level with her."

20:25, Bart, J. D., and the ruthless hoard arrived in the nation's capital. Another good night's sleep, and J. D. was off to Roanoke, Virginia. Three days of circumventing patrols and picket lines. It didn't matter much. Roanoke was disheveled from all the battles and skirmishes. As J. D. trotted down Main Street, he spied Mae's saddle on a beautiful Palomino tied up at the saloon/hotel. He stepped through the doorway, and a pair of familiar arms grabbed him and kissed him.

"Jay Malone, I am happy to see you!"

"It's good to see you too. What are you doing in Roanoke?"

"I will tell you upstairs." Mae dragged him up the stairs, opened the door to her room, pulled him inside, locked the door, and ripped every stitch of clothing off his body. "Jay, it's been months since I have been with a man. Kiss me!" After an hour of loving on one another, they took a break.

"Jay, what did you ask me before?"

"Oh, I was just curious why you are in Roanoke. This is the last place I expected to find you. Are you by yourself? Where are Luke and Tommy?"

"Down at the local whorehouse, where else?"

"Tommy too. I didn't think he went in for that sort of thing."

"He sure does now. Tom is long past the innocent teen you left months ago."

"Is that a bullet wound I felt on your right hip?"

"Yeah, it's all healed up now. Luckily, it went clean through. What the hell are you doing here?"

"I asked you first."

"Fair enough, we are on our way to D. C. to kill General Slaggart."

"Okay, who the hell is he?"

"My love, he is the idiot who gave Gen. Banks a field command, and he put Banks in charge of Fort Hays."

"Oh, that asshole. He really is an idiot, like you said."

"Okay, Jay, what are you doing here?"

"Looking for you. I missed you, honey. I wasn't sure if you would be happy to see me, after the disagreement we had in Toronto."

"I am sorry about the letter. I guess I just wanted you to know that I wasn't mad at you for not wanting to help me. Have you seen our wanted posters? We're famous. I haven't had to pay for a bottle of whiskey in quite some time. God, I am so glad you are here. Do you want to go to D.C. with us?"

"Sure, I am still not sold on what you are doing, but this guy sounds like a real shitbird. Have you had any close calls with the Union Army since the wanted posters showed up? How much am I worth? I was going for $1000."

"You are up to $1500 now. Luke and Tom are a little jealous. They are still only $1000 each."

"Sorry, I can't help them with that. How is Tom holding up in all this chaos?"

"I was worried he was going to start falling apart after he shot the soldier that put this hole in me, but now that he has discovered the opposite sex, he is distracted from all the killing going on around him."

"Mae, I have to ask, how long are you going to keep this up? How much revenge do you need?"

"Give me a break, Jay. You are starting to sound like Rev. Ames back home."

"Sorry, sweetheart, I had to ask. By the way, I heard a crazy story about you getting an honorary commission in the Confederate Army. Is that true?"

"Well, it turns out the boys in Richmond want to turn me into some kind of Confederate folk hero. They offered an honorary commission, making me a Lieutenant. I turned it down, of course. I despise Union Generals, but I absolutely refuse to condone any Army that tolerates slavery in any form. That's a big deal breaker for me."

"Even though killing Union Generals is aiding the Confederacy."

"Yes, I told you I have my own reasons for killing these arrogant assholes."

"Yeah, I guess you did. Where are you planning to kill Slaggart?"

"At his house in Washington, D.C.. You are coming with us, aren't you?"

"Yes, I guess I am officially back in the gang."

"Just remember one thing, lover, don't ever disappoint me again. Is that perfectly clear?"

"Crystal!"

"Do me a favor. Go down the street and round up Luke and Tom. They have been with those concubines long enough."

"Sure, be back in two shakes of a lamb's tail."

"Take your time. I need a little rest right now."

"Okay, is an hour long enough?"

"Yeah, that's perfect." J. D. walked out the door, down the stairs, and into the street. When the coast was clear, Major William Stuhill opened the linen closet door in Mae's room and closed it behind him. Mae looked Bill right square in the eye and said, "Are you dead sure J. D. is working for Feddelson and the War Department?"

"Yes, our spy in the War Department heard the conversation firsthand. They gave him a full pardon for the murder/kidnapping of Banks. Once the three of you are in federal custody, Malone is a free man. Oh yeah, he has a fiancée waiting for him up in Toronto when this is all over. Sucks to be her right now."

"That two-timing bastard. I'm gonna kill him myself!"

"Any ideas on how you want to ambush J. D. and his friends. You know good and well they will be waiting for us at the General's home. How many men do you have available to you right now?"

"I have four men at my command right now. That should be enough to eliminate Major Mackay's men. I heard they are all drunks. They won't be hard to compromise. When are you leaving for the capital?"

"Theirs or ours?"

"Theirs."

"We will be heading for Richmond in a day or two to get resupplied. There's nothing left in this town. Then it's off to Washington, D.C."

"Okay, but do me a favor, next time I'm in the linen closet, don't hump him so loud."

"Sorry, I got a little carried away. He's almost as good a lay as you are."

"Almost huh. Well, thank you for that. So, I guess I will see you in Richmond in three days." Will kissed Mae, slipped out the window, then scurried down the external stove pipe, making his undetected escape through the alley.

As instructed, J. D. walked three blocks north to Mrs. Mary's Emporium. Upon entering the establishment, he found himself surrounded by scantily clothed voluptuous women, thinking to himself, Wow! Then he inquired with the hostess, "Hello, I am looking for my friends Luke and Tom."

"Sir, I believe they are occupied at the moment. How can we serve you in the interim?"

"I would love a whiskey, thank you."

"Right away, sir."

"Your drink, sir. May I offer you something from our menu?" About a dozen women of gifted promiscuity began to sashay around right in front of him.

"Thank you, but I am just here to retrieve my friends."

"Another time perhaps?"

"Yes, possibly another time."

"We will look forward to serving you very soon. Excuse me, I will attempt to retrieve your cohorts for you."

"Thank you, I will help myself to another whiskey if you don't mind."

"Please, help yourself. Feel free to mingle with the other ladies." The hostess walked up a fancy flight of stairs and returned several minutes later with Luke and Tom. They both had huge smiles on their faces. Luke embraced J. D. and said, "What the hell are you doing here, buddy? I thought we had seen the last of you back in Toronto."

"Well, I guess I missed your Ma a little more than I realized. Hi Tom, how are you guys doing?"

Tom spoke up, "Fine, just fine! Especially as of about fifteen minutes ago. This place is amazing. Nothing but really fine whiskey and women."

"So, I noticed. Ma sent me to retrieve you guys. She is resting back in her room. Mae expects us to report back to her in about half an hour. I was just having a drink; do you want to join me for another round?"

"Sure. Tom, ask Miss Irene for two more glasses." Irene brought over more shot glasses and placed them on the table in front of the three men.

Tom interjected, "I can't believe you are really here. It ain't been the same since you left, what with Ma getting shot and all. She's been kind of moody and cranky without you around."

"She told me she got shot, and you killed the soldier that did it."

"Yeah, Luke and I shot him at the same time. The poor guy was probably dead before he hit the floor. This is a dirty business we are into right now. There ain't no turning back. Sometimes I really wonder if what we are doing is how respectable folks are supposed to act."

J. D. commented, "Tom, your mom has declared a personal war against these particular commanders because of their part in getting your family members killed. We are nothing but tools in the hands of the Almighty. Try not to get too caught up in the drama of it all. Just keep fighting. That's all any of us can do. And you are absolutely right; war is a very dirty business. All we can hope to do at this point is survive another day."

Luke retorted, "Do you really believe all that, or is it the whiskey talking?"

"Honestly, fellas, I think it's a little of both."

Tom commented, "I thought you didn't agree with Ma about this whole family vengeance thing. What made you change your mind?"

"Seeing my name on a wanted poster. That convinced me. When all this is said and done, we all could end up hanging at the end of a rope until we're dead. I still hope that knocking off a few more generals may cause the Union to consider suing for peace. That certainly can't hurt our situation. The more we represent ourselves as soldiers, the less likely we will be considered vigilantes."

"I never considered that, but I agree with Ma that the South's reason for fighting this war is dead wrong. I don't give 2 shits about states' rights, but slavery is just wrong."

J. D. illuded, "Look, Tom, sometimes self-preservation comes at a very high price. You have already had to kill a man to stay alive. I guarantee you that it will not be the last life you will take before all this is over. Drown your demons with whiskey if you have to, but don't stop fighting. Do that, and you are sure to lose everything: your family, friends, and your life. Come on, let's get out of here."

The three of them proceeded back to the hotel and rendezvoused with Mae. J. D. could not get past the fact that he may have to kill Tom, Luke, or Mae by the time this was over. That, he estimated, would be very difficult. The only thing that really kept him going was the thought of starting a new life in Toronto with Liz. Upon returning to the hotel, they discovered Mae was waiting for them in the lobby. "Well, boys, did you find solace and compassion in the arms of a stranger?"

Tom eagerly spoke up, "We sure did! I can't speak for Luke, but I did twice. I had to pay double, but it was worth every penny."

"I didn't need a detailed account of your carnal exploits; a simple yes would have sufficed."

Tom answered, "Well, yes, Ma, I did."

"Okay, gentlemen, let's go and get some supper. I am starving."

After a nice steak dinner, they hit the saloon and split a bottle of whiskey. Ma was noticeably quiet as J. D. proceeded to explain his sudden arrival in Roanoke. J. D. claimed to have spoken to an old friend and ex-U.S. Marshall friend of his. He was told by his ex-cohort approximately where they were. At this point, she knew full well that J.D. had sold out Mae and her sons for some kind of deal getting him off the hook for his part in the kidnapping. As Mae sat quietly listening to J. D.'s complete bullshit story, she became less and less compromised at the thought of killing the lying sack of cow dung with her bare hands. She postulated that when the opportunity presented itself, his death would be bloody and painful. *No man is going to get away with selling me out, even if he is a really good lay. I may be compelled to castrate the son of a bitch and watch him bleed out slowly.* After several rounds, Mae was ready for bed and proceeded to escort J. D. upstairs to her room for the night. There was no sense letting on about J. D.'s actual mission. Even Luke and Tom had absolutely no idea J. D. was a Union spy.

The next morning, just after dawn, Mae and her gang were back on the trail and headed for Richmond for some much-needed supplies. The most critical were flour and beans. Rifle cartridges were expensive but much less scarce at that point. Bacon was starting to run out as well.

As promised, the Quartermaster provided the flour, salt, and sow belly. An overnight bivouac just outside of town allowed for an early departure to Washington, D.C.

Chapter 19:
The Trap is Sprung

Major Mackay and his men had been posted outside Gen. Slaggert's private residence in the hope that he was Mae Anderson's next target. The General's mood was notably somber after learning that he was to be used as live bait to apprehend the Anderson Gang.

Jamie walked into the den where Grandpa was sitting in his favorite chair, reading the latest war dispatches.

"Grandpa, you are a general, is that right?"

"Yes, James, I am a two-star general commissioned in the Union Army."

"Have you been in a lot of battles?"

General Slaggert hesitated for a moment, cloaking the shame and embarrassment lurking behind his slightly cheerful disposition.

"James, you are ten going on eleven. What I am about to share with you must remain a private conversation, but I feel a sense of duty to you, my only grandson, nonetheless. I must confess to you that during my time as a division commander, I hated myself for the things I was forced to do on a daily basis. I was one of several senior field commanders who took part in the Battle of Antietam. A small body of water. Actually, it was nothing more than a creek. Still, no one could imagine at first glance that it would represent the bloodiest single-day battle in the war so far. I requested a transfer to the War Department here in Washington shortly after the battle. I had to; the death of my men was just too personal for me to bear. Thousands died that day. I followed my direct orders and sent my men out to die. For several nights following the battle, I would sit in my tent and agonize over the casualty lists my aides would bring to me. So many men, good men, Christian men, sacrificing themselves for a cause on both sides of the conflict. I would walk through and inspect the Hospital for several days after the battle. Wounded laying everywhere. Most would die an agonizing death in a very short time. It was such a waste of human spirit."

"Grandpa, you won the battle, right?"

"Technically, yes, but I ended up losing my soul. I am the catalyst for so many suffering family members who lost sons, uncles, fathers, and brothers. I gave the order. I stood and watched from an adjacent higher ground as the artillery exchanged volleys, churning up so much ground. Then the rifle exchange, followed by the bayonet charge. So many casualties. The dead and wounded seemed to parade by for miles. I have to remind myself that any and all of the soldiering I was called upon to perform was done in the service of my country as a means to an end, but that will not bring those men back from their hallowed battlefield graves. "It's as if I were wearing a mask to shield me from the brutal and chaotic task at hand. James, I implore you not to validate the illusion of battlefield glory. Please follow in your father's footsteps and pursue a law degree. Don't give yourself to the war machine."

"I will, Grandpa, if it means that much to you. Dad doesn't know it, but I have snuck into the courtroom when he is presenting a case. I like watching what he does."

"That's wonderful, nothing would please me greater than to see you graduate from the University with a law degree." James scampered back to the kitchen for a snack. The General opened the side drawer of his desk, revealing a loaded .44 cal. pistol, then promptly closed it back up. Immediately following that, he spoke to Major Mackay, in charge of his personal security detail.

"Major, my security detail is no longer needed. Report this to your commander at once. You and your men are officially relieved of this detail. Thank you for your prompt diligence in this matter. Dismissed!

"Sir, we have reports of the Anderson Gang listing you as their next target."

"Major, go ahead and report my request to command. If they feel it is warranted to continue, by all means, continue."

"Sir, yes, sir." Mackay gathered up his men and rode off to inform his commanding officer of the general's request. The general walked out into the foyer where his daughter was gathering hers and James's travel bags. He asked his daughter, Sarah, "Are you all packed for the trip back to Wilmington?"

"Yes, Dad. James and I had a wonderful visit. Did Maj. Mackay leaves already?"

"Yes, a slight change in priorities."

"Okay, I guess we will leave you to dwell in your solaced bachelorism once again."

She reached out to embrace him, and James came running through the front door. Then the three of them shared a big family hug.

"God, please grant you safe passage back home."

"Amen, Dad, and amen to you. Thank you for everything. Take very good care of yourself. Goodbye."

"Have a safe trip." As they rode out of sight down the long, winding driveway, he waved enthusiastically, knowing full well that he would never see them again. Turning back to walk into the house, he stopped and sat down in his favorite rocking chair, thinking to himself what of the afterlife I will yet to experience. I wonder if there are birds in heaven. Surely songbirds fill the air surrounding the resting place of eternal peace. Peace, something my conflict-riddled existence has seen very little of. I do pray for the peace of men's souls who have died so violently engaged in brutal, deadly combat. This war must come to a close at some point, but sadly, I will not live to see a non-combative end to this carnage. Steve stood up from his chair and returned to his study. He sat down at his desk and wrote a short goodbye letter to his loving family, apologizing for the irreversible act he would shortly commit. Then, with purposeful grit and determination, he reached into the drawer, removed his loaded service revolver, and placed the barrel slightly below his temple. "God grant me peace." He wrapped the index finger of his right hand around the trigger and squeezed a shot off. His lifeless body slid out of the chair and lay motionless on the floor.

It would be another twelve hours before his body was discovered by Major Mackay. Immediately after discovering the corpse, he set one of his men to dispatch a situation report to his commanding officer, Colonel Harrison. After reading the message, the Col. promptly exited his office and reported to Secretary Feddelson. He rebutted, "Suicide! Damn, I knew he was still distraught over Antietam, but I didn't see this one coming. Did he leave a suicide note?"

"Yes, sir, according to the message I received."

"Colonel, close my office door. Now this is exactly what you are going to do. I want you to return at once to the General's home and remove the service revolver he used and burn the suicide note. It is imperative that there is not a shred of evidence to indicate he took his own life. As far as the army is concerned, Mae Anderson shot him dead at his home. Do not attempt to apprehend her if and when she eventually arrives at his home, which should be as early as this evening, according to our latest update. to us. I want her to discover the body and sweat this one out for a while. See to it that all my instructions in this matter are carried out to the letter, and

Colonel! This conversation never took place. Is that absolutely clear?"

"Sir, yes, very clear, sir."

"Very well then, dismissed." Colonel Harrison rode immediately to General Slaggert's home to create the illusion of murder and remove any trace of the suicide which had recently transpired undetected to his superiors. The General's pistol was removed, and the suicide note was destroyed. The office was left slightly disheveled. Then he ordered Mackay and his men to shadow the movements of the Anderson's for the next several days.

The next morning, Mae and her gang approached the Slaggert home to discover no guard detail present. She sent J. D. and Luke out to scout the area for a possible ambush. Her men returned, reporting there was no trace of fresh tracks anywhere. J. D. said, "The only tracks we found away from the house were at least three or four days old. There is no one here."

Ma quipped, "I don't like this at all. Something's going on here. Tommy, go check out the house." Tommy rode up as close to the house under the cover of brush, then dismounted and approached the front porch on foot. Tom signaled for the others to advance. Once inside, they almost immediately discovered the body. J. D. figured he was shot in the last day or so. Ma was confused. Stuhill's latest information was that the General was relieved of command. He was put out to pasture, so why did they kill him? He wasn't the Confederate spy working in the War Department.

"Let's go, boys! We've been set up. Damn! They killed one of their own to frame us for it."

J. D. spoke up, "That dog won't hunt, Mae. The man probably offed himself and the Army wants us to take the fall. Either way, you are right, we need to get out of here fast."

The four of them headed north, arriving just south of Lancaster, Penn., around dusk. That's where they camped for the night to figure out their next move.

Mae asked, "Do any of you boys want coffee? We still have a couple of hours of daylight left." All of them responded favorably to her offer. After a hard ride, Mae's coffee is hard to beat, especially with a bourbon chaser. The four of them just sat around sipping their coffee and eating day-old biscuits from almost a week ago. By now, they were closer to hard-tack rations. It was a king's feast after a long day in the saddle. The wanted posters were starting to worry everyone. It had recently become very apparent that for at least three of them, it may not end well when all of this assassination business is said and done. The Union Army is finally learning how to fight, and the losses are starting to even out.

Mae spoke up, "Gentlemen, we are all thinking it, so I will just go out and say it. If the South doesn't win this war, we all may be prosecuted as vigilante war criminals, nothing but outlaws with a price on our heads."

Luke spoke up, "Ma, the army wants me for desertion, besides kidnapping and murder. My only real chance is to head for Mexico or Europe when this is all over."

Tom interjected, "Can't we just go back to California?"

J. D. quipped, "No, we would be spotted in no time anywhere out west. So far, every confederate town we have wandered into has been sympathetic to our cause, but money has a way of changing that. The only real chance we have of getting out of this alive is to find safe passage to Europe. I always fancied a trip to Ireland myself. That kind of traveling takes real money, though. We are well-heeled right now, but we're going to need lots more cash to sustain ourselves in Europe."

Ma retorted, "Okay, which do you prefer, banks or trains? Bear in mind, we are going to have to hit northern or western cities. The Confederate States are already struggling financially to keep up the war effort."

J. D. reluctantly answered, "Banks, of course, but honestly, wouldn't we be better going after Yankee payroll?"

Luke answered, "No, most of those payroll guard units are extremely well armed. We would need in excess of a hundred guns to pull off a caper that big."

Ma interjected, "So, we have decided to go after civilian Banks in northern states. Once we have amassed $25,000 in cash, we will secure passage to Ireland. Is that agreeable to everyone?" The men all nodded in agreement.

"Luke, you and J. D. should go and scout out Lancaster tomorrow morning. Oh, by the way, Luke, the local whorehouse is very rarely located in close proximity to the financial district, in case you were wondering. There will be no need to stop by there."

"Okay, Ma. I get it."

"No, not in Lancaster, you won't have time." A round of laughter ensued. Tom spoke, "Ma, do we really want to add bank robbery to our list of crimes. Couldn't we just start over in Europe with the money we have now?"

"Son, right now we only have a little over $1200.00 to get us through this. We need money fast. Right now, a bank is our best recourse to increase our stakes in Europe. I just hope Lancaster will be enough. If we have to knock over several banks, that will greatly lower our chances for success. Let's try and get some sleep. I have a feeling tomorrow is going to be a busy day for all of us."

Chapter 20:
A Nice Easy Bank Holdup

8:00 am. J. D. and Luke ride into Lancaster, entering from opposite ends so as to draw as little suspicion as possible. They met up at a restaurant for breakfast and shared a good, well-deserved meal. The first either had in almost a week. It was a Tuesday, so the bank would be working under normal business hours. It opened at 10 am sharp. The two men stepped inside and informed the teller that they wanted to open an account. Mr. Silkirk, the manager, escorted them into his office and processed their request.

J. D. asked, "Mr. Silkirk, is our $300.00 really going to be safe in this bank? There is a war on, you know, and we are just a couple of out-of-work blacksmiths looking for a job."

"I assure you, gentlemen, our bank is perfectly safe. We have a cable wire that runs directly to the Marshalls' Office three doors down. Any trouble and they are on their way."

"Well, sir, I personally will sleep better tonight having that information in my possession. We shouldn't take up any more of your time." Luke rode back to coordinate with Ma and Tom. J. D. stayed in town and spent the night in a local saloon/hotel. Luckily, he wasn't recognized in the saloon.

Luke arrived back at camp just prior to dusk. "Ma, this bank is easy pickings. The manager even told us about an alarm they had running to the Sheriff's Office. J. D. figures Tom and I should get the drop on the Sheriff and any deputies while you and J. D. hold up the bank."

"Okay, Luke, that sounds like a fairly good plan. What time does the bank open in the morning?"

"10 am sharp. I brought back some fresh salted pork and biscuits for all of us. Dig in." The three of them shared a nice little picnic before retiring for the night. Tom was still a little paranoid about robbing a bank in broad daylight. Somehow, he felt that something was bound to go wrong with tomorrow's caper. It just seemed too easy.

6:45 am. The boys woke up to the smell of bacon and fresh biscuits. They thought to themselves, *This is starting to look like a pretty good day, despite the prearranged criminal activity taking place at 10 am.* Ma was pouring the coffee as the boys were wrestling themselves out of their bedrolls. Luke said, "Boy, that coffee smells good. I am starving." Ma told everyone, "Dig in, fellas, we may have a long day ahead of us today after we hit the bank."

Luke retorted, "I think you are right about that. Ma, you want Tom and I to hold up the Sheriff's office at precisely the same moment you and J. D. are in the bank."

"Right, after J. D. and I are done in the bank, we will all head north for about five miles, then double back to this little hideout. We will cold camp for a day or two, then head for New Orleans to secure passage to Europe. The only tar in the molasses could be running the northern blockade down in the Gulf. Hopefully, we end up on a fast steamer. I guess we will cross that bridge when we get to it. Let's get ready to mount up. Ground everything you don't need. Pack the horses as light as you can so's to outrun the local posse." Shortly, the three of them rode together right into the heart of Lancaster. The time on the clock tower was 9:48, twelve minutes before the bank opened.

Luke and Tom quietly tied their horses in front of the Sheriff's office and proceeded to walk in through the door. The deputy at the desk asked in a rather serious tone, "What do you need, gentlemen?"

Luke spoke up as he drew his pistol, "Hands in the air. Now let me see your long johns."

Luke cocked his pistol and retorted, "Strip off your clothes now!" The deputy obliged immediately. Tom checked the brig for an empty jail cell. He opened the furthest one and ordered the deputy to enter. Once inside, Tom hogtied and gagged him, leaving the man lying on the bunk as he locked the cell door.

Luke said, "Okay, now we wait for the signal from the bank."

Three doors down the street, Mae and J. D. entered the bank while being welcomed by the clerk. Ma drew her shotgun and shoved it in the clerk's chest and told him, "Do exactly as I say, and you will live through this. Nod your head if you understand."

The clerk very quickly nodded his head to indicate yes. "Now call for the manager and then open up all the cash drawers right now."

The clerk called out, "Mr. Silkirk!" Immediately, Mae covered his mouth with her hand and whispered, "Shush."

Silkirk exited his office. J. D. immediately pushed the barrel of his revolver into the man's back and said, "Good morning, sir, I would like to withdraw my three hundred dollars from your bank along with interest. Open the safe and fill up the carpet bags now!"

Silkirk said, "You will never get away with this. The sheriff will hunt you down like a dog." J. D. cocked his pistol and answered, "You let us worry about your sheriff, just keep filling up those bags with all the cash and coins." After Silkirk was finished cleaning out the safe J. D. hogtied and gagged both men. Just before exiting the bank J. D. pulled the alarm, alerting Luke and Tom that it was time to go. All four of them mounted their horses and rode quietly out of town on the northbound trail.

After doubling back, they headed for the camp south of town, some twenty miles away. No posse in sight. Either they continued north or were too far behind to catch up. Either way, there was no one closely trailing them from Lancaster.

After arriving back at camp, they immediately started counting their haul from the robbery. Ten minutes later, the combined amount was over $20,000 in cash and over $18,000 in gold coins. They were barely halfway through it all. When it was all counted, they realized they had gotten away with $37,000 in cash and another $28,000 in gold. Taking into account the gold at face value. They hit the right bank at just the right time. "Holy shit, boys, we're rich!!"

"Pipe down, Ma," J. D. whispered. "This is too much money. The town is going to post a huge reward for this. We have got to get to Virginia fast. Every two-bit bounty hunter in the territory is going to be gunning for us. We should forget New Orleans and head for Charleston to embark for Ireland. Also, this is too much gold to carry around in carpet and saddle bags. We are going to need travel trunks. All of us are going to have to look like a wealthy aristocratic family if we plan to get out of here alive. I'm talking new identities, clothes, mannerisms, everything. We could assume the identity of a dead person. There was a wealthy family from Texas that was killed in an unfortunate house fire. They had two sons of Tom's age. I think we should call ourselves the Winslows. Sarah, Bill, Shawn, and Beauregard. Beau for short. That should get us on the boat anyway. If we split up now, we would have a better chance of getting to Charleston undetected."

Mae interjected, "Okay. I just have one question. Will Major Mackay and his crew be there to greet us properly when we arrive?"

In a very somber voice, J. D. answered, "How long have you known about Mackay and his boys?"

Mae pulled her sidearm and said, "Tom, take his pistol belt and the derringer in his boot, plus anything else he has concealed."

"Right away, Ma."

"Now, J. D., answer my question."

"I am sorry, but they made me do it. I was facing twenty years of hard labor. It seemed like my only way out. As for your question, no! Mackay knows nothing about the robbery. He is waiting for us in Buffalo, NY. The Union wants us alive so they can put you and the boys on trial for the murder of Banks and now Slaggert too. That was the deal. I was to receive a full pardon in exchange for expediting your capture. You got too believe me when I tell you I had absolutely no intention of going through with it. The whole thing stunk right from the beginning. I was just waiting for the best opportunity to lead them away from us. As soon as they hear we hit that bank in Landcaster, they are going to know I flipped on the deal. I was planning to come clean about everything on the boat."

Mae walked closer to J. D. while holstering her pistol. "Darling, I want to believe you." She slowly drew a roach belly blade from her apron and ran it right into his chest, penetrating his heart and lung area. His body fell to the ground. "But I just can't take that chance."

Luke, take his body off in the woods and conceal it so it won't be discovered for quite some time." Luke picked up what was left of J. D. and threw it over the pack horse and mounted his. Then he led both horses away. Tom watched as Luke disappeared into the deep surrounding woods.

Tom uttered, "You're a hard woman, Ma."

"I told you kid. You have to be that way to survive in this world. The only people I trust right now are Luke and you. At this point, we are all that each other has. Go ahead and eat something, boy. The journey to New Orleans ain't going to be easy like Luke said.

We will have to keep our wits about us at all times. When Luke gets back, we will get all this loot ready for travel. I don't think we will have much trouble getting there if we don't bring any attention to ourselves along the way."

Chapter 21:
All Aboard for Havana

The trek to New Orleans proved to be very treacherous with the Union Army of the Potomac scattered across two states, blocking most of the main southern thoroughfares to the Carolinas. Safe passage would require mirroring the Appalachian Trail almost into the Arkansas Ozarks. The journey would take almost seven weeks and require much sacrifice on the gang's part. They would have to rely on obscure trading posts for supplies. Baths came in the form of cold mountain streams, but necessary to keep up morale between them. Getting clean, body and garments, even in a brisk stream, felt pretty good after a long day on horseback. There was enough melancholy to go around by the time the gang reached the Ozarks. Talk around the campfire always led back to the family farm in Missouri. Some evenings, it was all that Mae could tolerate.

"Boys, I miss our old life back in Missouri as much as you do, more in fact. Tom and I settled there before you boys started showing up. Your daddy was a good man. Not a God-fearing man, but he had his priorities in the right place. We literally built that farm from the ground up. The church neighbors pitched in to frame the buildings, but the job of raising you bunch of knot heads, and securing a successful business raising livestock fell upon the two of us. Many days, Tom worked well after nine o'clock, came in for a late supper, went to bed, and started again at five o'clock the next morning.

People used to scoff at Tom because of his peculiar Sunday morning benders. I say he earned the right to let off a little steam when the farm started to turn a nice profit. All those Monday morning hypocrites were at our auction every year, gambling, boozing, etc. The Rev. Ames included."

"Ma, Tom, and I never saw anyone speak ill of Pa while he was dropping us off."

"Of course, not, son, that would be a gossip coming from the devil's own lips. They waited until Monday to talk all their trash about us. Well, I will let you in on a little secret. Our farm and auction kept those folks thriving, even during so-called depressions. They all owe their very survivability before the war to every one of us."

"Ma, Luke, and I want to know the whole story. Why did you kill J. D. right in front of us, the way you did? You owe us that much at least."

"It ain't easy to explain. I guess I just couldn't trust him anymore. I have known that J. D. was plotting against us ever since we met him in Roanoke. Stuhill found out from a spy working at the Union War Department in D. C. I really wanted to believe him, but when he talked about heading to Charleston for passage to Ireland, I knew there was no way he had any intention of going to Europe. We never would have made it through the Shenandoah Valley without being caught. Then there is the little matter of his girlfriend/fiancée waiting piously for his safe return into her young arms. He didn't wait very long to shack up with some other little tart. Yes, trust issues and scorn got that man a blade in the chest. End of story. Any more questions?" A pair of curt no's echoed through the trees.

"Boys, we had better split up when we get to New Orleans. I will try and secure us passage on a steamer or clipper. Preferably a steamer. The trip will be much shorter aboard one of those. You two scout the town. Make sure there are no handbills on us anywhere.

Another thing. We should definitely travel under an alias. We will use the name J. D. suggested. So, we are now the Winslows: Sarah, Sean, and Beau, raised from the depths of their house fire. We should arrive there at noon tomorrow. I will find us a real nice hotel to stay in. Let's plan to meet up again in the French Quarter at 2 o'clock tomorrow afternoon. There has to be a bar or saloon down there somewhere. Then we get to go shopping for new duds after we find a decent bathhouse to get washed up. Sean, formerly Luke, answered, "Okay, Ma, that sounds like a good plan."

New Orleans was showing signs of despair in the despondent people still living there. The war was starting to wreak havoc throughout. Once the city was under complete control of the Union Command, martial law was declared. Sean rode slowly past the Marshall's office on his way to the French Quarter. One of the several wanted posters attached to the outside of the building was of the Anderson Gang, with a bounty of $7000.00 for the three of them, dead or alive. Sean trotted off as quietly as he could. The place was crawling with Yankee soldiers and lawmen.

Ma and Beau caught sight of one another in front of a saloon on Bourbon St. They dismounted, tied up their horses, and walked inside. About ten minutes later, Sean walked in and sat at a table right next to them. He reached back in his chair within earshot of Sarah, Then Whispered, "We have to get the hell out of here. Our faces are all over this town. The bounty on the three of us is $7000.00. They're offering 5 grand for you alone."

"Okay, let's go get cleaned up at the bath house across the street. Beau and I will meet you there in five minutes." After a hot bath and a boiled wash, they headed down the street to purchase new clothing. The next stop was to a livery stable to trade their horses for a family-sized buggy to get around in.

Peter Mann was the proprietor of Mann's Livery. He just happened to see them approaching on the street and waved them over. Once inside his stable, he quickly closed the door. "As I live and breathe! The Anderson Gang is in my stable. Pardon my asking, but what the hell are you doing down here? Half the city knows about the bounty on you folks. You are hotter than a bowl of jambalaya right now."

Ma spoke up, "We are headed for Ireland on a Steamer leaving tomorrow morning. Boarding starts at 6 o'clock this evening."

"What is the name of the boat?'

"The Fanning Star."

Peter continued, "Okay, that is Capt. Williams boat. You may have a chance. He has absolutely no sympathy for the Yankees, I can tell you that much. As long as there are no spies in his crew, you may make it out of here."

Ma asked, "Peter, we need a buggy or a wagon to get our grip to the dock."

"Yes. I have a covered wagon that should do nicely. If you want, I will deliver you there myself."

"Don't put yourself out on our account. I would hate for you to be wrapped up in our mess."

"Don't fret about that, the Capt. and I go way back. We fought the British together in 1812. That's a story for another time."

Peter and the boys loaded their travel trunk and carpet bags in the wagon, then headed for the wharf. Getting to the loading dock was easy. Peter escorted them to the first mate, Mr. Gadson. He then showed them to their cabin and presented Ma with the key. She opened the door and was greeted with five loaded revolvers.

Major Mackay said, "Welcome to New Orleans, Mae. Everyone, come on in." Mackay's men proceeded to frisk and disarm her and the boys, followed by dawning them in shackles. "Sorry about the shackles, but you three are slipperier than a rattler covered in bear grease, and twice as dangerous. So, where is Josiah?"

Ma told Mackay, "We left him in Pennsylvania."

"Was he dead or alive? No matter, it's the three of you the War Dept. is after, not him. Now, all of us are going to take a nice, easy boat ride to Washington, D.C. Any of you step out of line at all during the trip, and I swear on my mother's grave, I will give you over to my deputies and turn my back.

Let me tell you, these men will fight amongst themselves to see who gets to draw and quarter the lot of you. They are not civilized men. As long as I say, you are to receive good treatment for the entire journey. Oh, yes, I almost forgot, my boys and I will get fifteen cents on the dollar for every penny we return to Lancaster, in addition to a bonus for bringing all of you in alive. I have to admit that was awfully slick how you pulled that caper off in broad daylight. They didn't discover the poor deputy, the clerk, and the bank owner until three hours later. The sheriff didn't even bother sending out a posse. He sent a wire to the War Department telling them what happened. Honestly, we lost track of you in Virginia, but after the bank job, we were able to pick up your trail. I was puzzled at first why you didn't just head for the Yukon and take your chances with the Mounties. At that point, I knew I would never catch you heading south over the Appalachians, so I secured maritime passage for my men and me to New Orleans. When you were spotted outside of Memphis, I was convinced you would show up in New Orleans or Pensacola sooner or later. Okay, if you have nothing to add, then we will disembark and switch boats. The Frigate that we will be traveling on is not going to be nearly as accommodating for you as it will for me. Alright, let's go out the door single file."

"Major, I do have a request. I would like permission to send a wire to my other two sons if they are still alive. Would that be possible?"

"Yes, Mae, I can take care of that before we leave New Orleans. What do you want to tell them?"

"Thank you for that. Just send 'Arrested in New Orleans for a murder committed in Kansas, headed to Washington D. C. for the arraignment. Love Ma."

"Don't forget about Virginia."

"We didn't kill that bastard. He was already dead when we got there."

"Not according to my bosses."

Luke spoke up, "Those lying bunch of snakes."

"Just one snake, Secretary of War Feddelson. He is mighty pissed off about the whole damn thing. We should arrive in D. C. three to four days from now. Hopefully, the message gets to your kin fairly soon. For what it's worth, I think you are being used so that the Army can save face and not publicly admit that the General committed suicide. In this instance, you are a resource being used. Nobody is going to give one speck of a damn what you say. Okay, people, let's get going."

Chapter 22:
Captured

Mackay and his men escorted what was left of the gang to the Frigate Sacramento, where they were promptly housed in the ship's brig and kept under heavy 24-hour guard. The blacksmith was telling the truth when he said that everyone in New Orleans knew that the Andersons were en route. Mackay had union collaborators all over the city, recruited by the local law enforcement agencies. There was no way Mae and the boys were going to slip through.

Soon after the boat left New Orleans for Washington D. C., Mae was informed that dispatches were sent to her other two sons. Mackay also told Mae that they were en route to D. C. The cruise took about four days. The prisoners, Mae, Luke, and Tom, being the only passengers, were given main deck privileges when the weather was fair. In fact, the crew was quite taken by Mae's charm and charisma. Still, she and the boys were shackled about the wrist and ankles for the entire journey.

Upon arrival, the boat was moored in the Potomac River. Mackay then brought the prisoners directly to the Old Capitol Prison, where they remained until their subsequent arraignment and federal trial. Ma, Luke, and Tom were put in separate solitary cells for twenty-one hours a day. They were given three hours a day to commune together with their legal counsel. Upon arrival, their legal team consisted of three first-year military attorneys, who immediately recommended pleading guilty to all charges to avoid a death sentence. But honestly, their lawyers could not guarantee that the three of them wouldn't be hanged anyway. Still, it seemed a viable alternative considering pleas of not guilty would most assuredly guarantee a trip to the gallows.

The most promising defense strategy was to try to convince the court that the Anderson Gang represented a private militia that should be given all the rights and privileges awarded to Confederate soldiers. The major problems with that defense were that there was no actual documentation connecting the Andersons with the Confederacy at any level. The only way that their actions benefited the South was in creating short-term chaos by replacing the dead field commanders. Mae and the boys saw from very early on that an appointment with their executioners was to be their destiny. Several motions were filed for civilian trials in the respective states, knowing full well that the Attorney Generals in Tennessee and Virginia would not even serve warrants for the Andersons' Arrest. The Union Army wanted their pound of flesh out of every one of them; there was absolutely no way that they would ever see the inside of a civilian courtroom before this was complete. The Secretary of War wanted to put a stop to any notion of valor in destroying the enemies of the Confederacy by the Andersons.

Approximately two weeks later, Matthew and Mark arrived at the prison. They were immediately given complete access to their family members. The reunion was somber at best. The last time Mark and Luke had seen Ma and their younger brothers was the morning they headed for Chicago to enlist in the Union Army.

Upon seeing her two oldest sons ride through the courtyard en route to the solitary confinement cells, she wept uncontrollably from the inside of her cell. It was all Mae could do to control her emotions. She was astonishingly embarrassed by her actions that led to her family's situation. She and two of her remaining sons were going to die like common, desperate outlaws. Maybe if she alone pled guilty to all charges, Luke and Tom could be spared. After a subsequent hour of melancholy and remorse, Mae finally found the stamina to greet Matthew and Mark properly, with only an occasional tear and regretful sigh. Mark spoke up first, "Ma, how are you doing here? Are they treating you well? Do you have enough to eat and drink?"

"Yes, boys, your mother is being treated as kindly and fairly as I could expect, considering my situation. The soldiers who are in charge of my care have been respectful and professional ever since we arrived here. Your brothers and I are only shackled when being escorted to and from our cells for meals and personal time. I am very happy to see you both. I only wish it were in better circumstances." Matthew asked, "Why did you allegedly do what they are accusing you of?"

"Wow, now you sound like my baby-faced Army lawyer. Okay. I will tell you what you want to know. I did it to avenge the dead. All the soldiers who lay where they were slain on every battlefield in this ridiculous, bloody, chaotic war. This conflict will solve nothing. The hate and prejudices will continue far beyond any resolution signed as a means to an end. As a widow and mother of slain children, I share a heartache and loss with other women in my situation that no man could ever comprehend. My husband was taken from me. He was the man I created John and Andrew with. Subsequently, He was killed prior to either of them. I alone, as the woman who gave life to these men, suffered the agonies of a permanent separation. God will never cause more suffering than anyone can bear, but having to face the loss of a child creates an emptiness in a mother's soul likened to earthly damnation. I am angry! I am scorned. I constantly perspire hate toward these men who treat death like a game of chess. Pieces flung about to eventually find the endgame. I am sure I will holler like a demon in hell for my sins, I just hope my actions may have eased the suffering of other madres.

Does that answer your question, son?"

"Completely!"

"Mark, you are very quiet today. Did I shock you with my revelation?"

"Yes, quite. My chosen profession allows me the courtesy or privilege to search for good anywhere it is lacking. I strive to create a balance for the suffering by casting light onto shadowed souls through hope, faith, and the promise of eternal peace through the acceptance of Christ in their hearts. I fear the darkness shadowing your soul will take many days for the light to penetrate. Right now, there is a massive amount of indifference blinding your ability to forgive."

"You always were a very charismatic spokesman. Those were eloquent words, but I made my peace with God prior to starting this quest for revenge. I have accepted my fate."

Mark concluded, "Ma, I will continue to pray for you, Tom, and Luke for as long as possible. What could it possibly hurt at this point?"

Ma told him, "Nothing, I suppose." The guard announced, "Time!" Matthew and Mark were escorted out of the brig and headed over to the defense attorney's office to make inquiries.

The two older brothers entered The Judge Advocate General's Office and were directed to Captain Cummings, head of The Anderson's legal defense team. Once inside the office, Capt. Cumings asked them to have a seat and make themselves comfortable.

"Gentlemen, I am glad you found your way to my office. Have you had a chance to visit with your incarcerated family members yet?"

Mark spoke up, "Yes, we just came from the brig."

"Good, then you know how absolutely serious these charges are. I must tell you frankly, their best defense is to plead guilty and throw themselves upon the mercy of the court. This may possibly save Thomas's life. There is no way Mae and Luke will escape the death penalty. Thomas is barely eighteen. The conversations I have had with the Tribunal members have alluded to a lighter sentence for the young man. Unfortunately, he may receive up to thirty years of hard labor. He will serve his sentence, or possibly get released early for good behavior, then move on with his life.

As for Luke, even considering his excellent war record prior to the incident at Fort Hays will not be anywhere near enough to keep him from being hanged. He will be executed for desertion. Never mind the charges of accessory to murder and kidnapping. Your mother's fate was sealed the minute she decided to start killing generals. I must convey to you that there is a huge amount of resentment for her in this building alone. I don't want to tell you what the War Dept. thinks of her right now."

Matt answered, "Yes, we can assume that Sec. Feddelson can't wait for her execution."

"That's about the size of it."

Mark asked, "Have they set a date for the arraignment and trial yet?"

"Yes, the arraignment was last week. As I eluded to, they only charged Thomas with manslaughter and accessory to kidnapping. If his sentences run concurrently, he could get as little as ten years, probably hard labor. It would appear that his boyish appearance has softened the Tribunal's scorn toward him. That will not be the case for Luke and your Mom. They both face a plethora of capitol felony charges, including murder, kidnapping, treason, etc. At the arraignment, all three of them attempted to plead 'no contest,' but the president of the tribunal refused to accept it. We have until this coming Monday to enter another plea. Tom and Luke will plead guilty to all charges. Mae still wants to plead not guilty, but we are still working on that. Today is Thursday, and we have until Monday morning at 1000 hrs. to convince her otherwise. I was hoping the two of you could help us in that respect. I have an appointment with them tomorrow morning at 0900 hrs. I would like both of you to be there. I was counting on both of you for character references in the form of written affidavits to present to the court prior to sentencing. Could you have them ready by Monday morning?"

Matt and Mark both agreed. "Okay, if there aren't any other questions, gentlemen, I will see you tomorrow morning."

Matt and Mark headed for the post library to write the affidavits requested by Capt. Cummings. Upon entering the library, they both sat down in the reference section and began to write and talk among themselves. "Mark, I think we should concentrate on separate areas of their characters. I will focus on philanthropy and leave any religious rhetoric to you."

"Matt, I hate to point out the fact that, given the nature of these charges, it would be very difficult to spin their characters and show any religious value to their actions. I think we should concentrate on philanthropy and generosity to achieve any sympathy for their case."

"Point well taken, brother. Yes, we don't want to get into a spiritual argument for which we are sure to lose. We should definitely center around Ma's giving nature, always giving leftovers to the orphans when she ran the restaurant back home. We could also mention the anguish that a mother suffers in having to bury a child."

"Good, let's stick to that."

"Mark, I don't want to spoil anyone's picnic, but I think we are probably trying to grow teats on a bull here. If we look at this thing logically, it seems quite clear that Ma and Luke are going to be executed forthwith. But, and this is a big but, we may be able to get Tommy's sentence reduced to exclude hard labor. I will pen the affidavit for Ma and Luke. You write the one for Tommy."

"Yes, hopefully writing separate letters will somehow shield the heinousness of the act from little brother. Let's get started." Both men worked well into the night, discarding draft after draft. Finally, at close to midnight, the deed was done. After the brothers had proofed the others' letter, it was agreed that they just may have averted a miserable life of institutionalization for Tommy.

Chapter 23:
A Solaced Reunion

Friday morning saw another meeting for the accused with their legal counsel, along with the two older brothers. Capt. Cummings read the letters prepared by Matt and Mark. He further commented, "Very good, gentlemen. I don't honestly know how much weight they will carry with the Generals, but they are both eloquent and to the point. Thank you."

"Now, Mae, have you reconsidered changing your plea to guilty?"

"If it will help Tommy avoid a hanging, then yes, I will switch to guilty."

"Good! So, Monday morning, we will address the tribunal and change your pleas to guilty."

Mae asked, "Capt. will they sentence us then?"

"No, I do not believe so. The president of the court-martial will want to have a sit-down with Secretary Feddelson before passing sentence. The court should reconvene in a week to ten days after the hearing. I should prepare you all for the very real possibility of the death penalty for all three of you. As of now, I believe it is off the table for Tom, but Feddelson has been on a tirade over this entire campaign. I honestly don't know which way he will decide on this one."

Monday morning at 0955 hrs. saw a very busy courtroom. Mostly filled with the press agents. The trial was drawing headlines across the country, especially in the Confederate States. The Anderson Gang vs The U.S. Army. This proceeding was being documented vicariously as a fight between armed combatants, eerily similar to previous battles leading up to these court appearances.

The Sgt. of Arms announced, "Attention!" The tribunal entered the room and ordered everyone to be seated. The prosecution listed the charges. President of the tribunal, General Percival Smith, asked the defense counsel if they wanted to change their plea. All three of the accused said, "Guilty!"

Capt. Cummings interjected, "General sir, I would like to make a motion to have character witness affidavits placed into the court records prepared by Capt. Matthew Anderson and Lt. Mark Anderson on behalf of Mae, Luke, and Thomas Anderson."

"So noted. Place them in the court records. Additionally," General Smith announced, "Let the record indicate each of the accused entered a plea of guilty to the charges in question. This court-martial will reconvene in ten days for sentencing. This hearing is adjourned." The courtroom was cleared, and the prisoners were escorted back to the brig.

The next morning, at the request of Sec. Feddelson, General Smith left with his staff for the office of the War Dept. Upon arriving, Gen. Smith was escorted to Sec. Feddelson's office. Immediately after entering the office, Feddelson walked from behind his desk to shake hands with his old friend from the academy. "Percy, come on in, you old warhorse. Get yourself in here and have a chair. Do you want a whiskey to whet your whistle?"

"Sure, Bill. make it a tall one, the trip getting here was really dusty."

"So, you got them to plead guilty to all of the charges. Excellent work! When did you schedule the hangings?"

"Sentencing is not for another nine days. Actually, I wanted to talk to you about that. the younger brother. Thomas Jr. pled guilty to accessory to kidnapping and manslaughter. I feel he should be sentenced to 10 years without parole. Only Mae and Luke Anderson should be hung."

Bill sarcastically quipped, "That is very sweet, Percy." In a more serious tone, he rebutted, "But forget it, I want him hung like the other two."

"Bill, I know you are genuinely pissed off about the entire situation, but listen to reason. Ma was calling the shots from the very beginning; Tom is only eighteen years old. Remember our first year in the Academy. We were the same age as him. I am all for hanging the other two. They are both getting exactly what they deserve. I'm not saying the kid is innocent by any stretch of the imagination, but I don't like putting this young man in the same category with the others. Let him rot in a cell for ten years. No chance for parole or early release for good behavior. He does the full term. No one will accuse us of being soft on vigilantes. If anything, the press may see it as a good thing. Honestly, our case against Thomas wasn't that concrete. There was the possibility that he could have been acquitted if the case had gone to trial. We have the other two dead to rights. Everyone wants to see Mae hang for murder and Luke hang for desertion. There's your two pounds of flesh."

"Are you finished? You can come from behind that pulpit and listen for one moment. Look, I know exactly how old the young man is. I know he is just a kid, but he was old enough to make his own decision when Mae Anderson started on this campaign of revenge. Our intelligence was very reliable. They were all in this together. Don't forget the bank job they pulled off in Lancaster. Look, I know the money was recovered and given back to the bank minus the finder's fee. Hell, the bank owner didn't even press charges. He expects us to do our duty and hang the bastard. How can we let him off like that?"

"Bill, you owe me. You would not be sitting in that chair sipping on finely aged whiskey every day if I had not covered your ass at least a dozen times over the years. Remember when I stood your watch on guard duty while you were playing patty cake with our commanding officer's daughter. Or how about the fire in the ordinance bunker down in Austin, Texas? All duty rosters miraculously burned up in the same fire. You owe me big time, buddy. Now I am calling in one of those markers."

"Okay, dammit, you win. Throw the kid in prison. Percy, sometimes you can be a real hard ass."

"Bill, you know it is the right thing to do."

"Yeah, well, I just hope the old man in the White House thinks the same way you do, or I will end up having to listen to his ranting rhetoric for hours on end." The two men went back to sipping whiskey and reminiscing about their exploits as young junior officers.

Chapter 24:
A Date With Destiny

There was an extreme hush throughout the courtroom as General Smith ordered the Andersons to stand and hear their sentence. The General glared into Mae's piercing blue hazel eyes and said, "Mae Anderson, by your own admission, this Tribunal finds you guilty of four counts of first-degree murder and sentences you to be hanged by the neck until you are dead. Sentence to be carried out thirty days from today at this location. You will remain incarcerated at this facility until your execution.

Luke Anderson, by your own admission, this Tribunal finds you guilty of Treason against the United States of America, Desertion against the United States Army, and one count of first-degree murder. Furthermore, you are sentenced to be hanged by the neck until you are dead. Sentence to be carried out thirty days from today at this location. You will remain incarcerated in this facility until your execution.

Thomas Anderson Jr., by your own admission, this Tribunal finds you guilty of accessory to kidnapping and manslaughter. You are hereby sentenced to remain incarcerated for ten years in a federal prison with no possibility of early release."

A blissful sigh of relief fell over the room, with family members sobbing. The united, unmistakable thought on everyone's mind is, 'Yes, the boy gets to live.'

"Sentence to begin immediately following this procession. Your incarceration will take place at this facility. This concludes all matters in the case of The United States vs The Anderson Gang. Dismissed!"

General Smith left the courtroom and walked back to his VIP quarters, and closed the door behind him as he walked inside. He grabbed a shot glass and the whisky bottle above the hearth. Then he sat down and proceeded to get really drunk. As the alcohol rolled off his tongue and down his throat with a warm burning sensation, he murmured out loud, "It never gets any easier, sentencing people to die. The boy isn't going to be executed. I guess that accounts for something." Percy slipped off his boots and leaned back in his chair, letting out a prayerful sigh, thanking the almighty that his ordeal with the Andersons was over. The whiskey had done its job as he nodded off to sleep in his chair.

As the date of execution started to draw near, Mae and Luke took some comfort from Mark and his unwavering spiritual guidance. The Sgt. of the Guard kept Mae and Luke's inner cells unlocked during the day. There was an unwavering awareness that the coming executions were different. Mae was a beautiful middle-aged woman who, given normal circumstances, would be joyous and full of life.

The final week prior to their appointment with the hangman, neither Mae nor Luke would set foot outside the brig. They did not want to have to look at the device built especially for their demise. A wooden platform reeking of cold, callous death. It is the devil's altar. A portal capturing human souls for Lucifer. Suffered playthings under a demon's beck and call.

As the end of her days approached, Ma didn't really want to socialize with us boys. The Sgt. of the Guard allowed the entire family to be together for several hours every day, but Ma didn't join in very often. During the time that was left for her and Luke, Ma would remain reticent in her cell, contemplating the many abominations she would be confronted with when eventually meeting with Satan face to face. Even her substantial Quaker upbringing could not grant any peace at this moment.

Private Combs walked by Mae's cell and uttered in a very sincere voice. "I have been praying for you, Ma'am. Every night. Many of us privates pray for you.

It may not be my place to say this, Ma'am, but I think you are too young to die, and at the end of a rope. It just doesn't seem proper."

"Private Combs, what is your first name?"

"Luther, Ma'am. My folks named me Luther on account of that fancy preacher over in England or somewhere abouts there."

"It's a pleasure to meet you, Luther. I find no grandeur in telling you I am a woman scorned. I killed those men because they wronged my family and me. I felt no other recourse but to seek revenge. Now, after my crops are planted. The yield of my harvest is a bitter reflection of ugliness and shame. I deserve to die, and death by hanging suits my crime. I felt as if I was striking a blow for war widows and children left without a husband or father to depend on. War is the devil's playground, and men are drawn to it like bees to honey. Men dream of the glory of battle, medals of valor bravely pinned right to their chest, and the ranked significance of multiple battle scars. Those scars run deep, my young, naive friend. Consider the fallen at Gettysburg, less than two months ago. There is no valor, only unmarked graves for thousands of men and horses."

"My brother was in that battle. He took a mini ball in his right shoulder. The war is over for him. I got a letter from Ma last week. I am scheduled to join a combat unit as soon as they han… I am sorry, Ma'am; I meant no disrespect."

"It's okay, Luther, I know my judgement day is vastly approaching." A gruff voice rang out down the corridor, "Combs!"

"Skuse me Mam. Right away, Sarge!" Private Combs scurried back to the Sgt. of the Guard ASAP. It was time for the changing of the guard. Private Dill would stand at his post for the next four hours. Dill was all business and not too much of a talker. Mae lay back on her lumpy mattress stuffed with alfalfa hay and stared up at the ceiling joists in front of her. They were not unlike the ones in the first cabin that she and Thomas Sr. built together in Missouri. Her thoughts wandered back to passionate incidents of warm consummating embraces that would last well into the night. In that moment, she was consumed with sweet memories of not so long ago and slowly drifted off to sleep.

Hours later, Mae was awake to the abrupt sound of what she mistakenly thought was roaring thunder. Peering outside the small window of her cell, she was cauterized by the reality of counterweight sandbags falling abruptly through the hangman's platform. A harsh reality to such a short, blissful daydream. She stood there in awe, watching the Hangman ply his trade. All she could hope for at this point was a quick and relatively pain-free death. Mae ventured into the larger holding cell where all of her sons were sitting around a crude dining table engaged in boisterous camaraderie. Mae hugged them all, one by one, and sat down at the head of the table. "So, boys, is it surf and turf again? I hope not. You know how that rich food gives me the gas something awful." Then she raised her right buttocks slightly and squeezed out a slight burp. A round of jolly laughter followed.

Mae asked, "Did Capt. Cummings pay us a visit today? I was wondering how our appeal went."

Matthew said, "The appeal to the White House has fallen on deaf ears. There will be no stay of execution for either of you. Your hangings are in five days. There are no legal avenues available to stop that from happening now." Mark intervened during the morbidly somber moment with a prayer.

"God, in heaven, please watch over us in our greatest hour of need. Oh, great God of mercy, ease our pain and strife as Ma and Luke face their final judgement upon this earth. Allow our hearts to be softened by the love and respect that we all share for thee. We humbly bow and respectfully beg for your divine grace upon us all. Lovingly in Christ's name, amen." Tom commented, "That was beautiful, brother. I sincerely thank you for that. If there is a God in heaven, I pray he watches over me during my time here."

Ma spoke, "Tom, my ever-dutiful son. You may endure many unspeakable hardships during your incarceration. Remember this very well. All you have to do is survive. Do the ten years and move on to another chapter of your life, or just as sure as sunrise, I will come back to haunt your ass for the rest of your life."

"Yes, Ma'am!"

"Good. When they let you out, go find your brothers and start over. You know the mercantile business; change your name and find an opportunity." Mark interjected, "Tom, Matthew, and I have agreed to keep tabs on you while you're here. Just don't pick up any bad vices, and you will make it."

Chapter 25:
Two Coffins

0700 hrs. on the fatal day. Mae and Luke gave their requests for the last meal. Steak and lobster, baked beans, and biscuits with honey. The Sgt. of the Guard informed them that their sentence would commence two hours after receiving their final meal at approximately 0900 hrs.

The post Chaplin, Lt. Earls, accompanied Mark and Matthew for a final visit prior to the sentence being carried out. Lt. Earls was very respectful of Mae and Luke. He did not attempt to tarnish the family's final moments together in any way. At 1045 hrs., the Sgt. of the Guard walked down to the large holding cell and announced in a very respectful voice, "Sirs, it's time. I must escort all family members outside." Matthew answered, "Yes, thank you, Sgt."

Everyone stood up from their chairs and took their final embraces. Tom was escorted to his cell. Mark and I walked outside the brig and saluted the post commander, Colonel Bridges, as he was en route to escort the prisoners to the gallows. As the colonel entered the brig, the duty Sergeant announced, "Attention!" Colonel Bridges spoke, "At ease, Sgt. Are the prisoners ready?"

"They are being shackled as we speak, sir. The prisoners will be ready in just a few moments."

"Very good, Sgt. I, Lt. Earls, and you, along with two armed guards, will march the prisoners to the platform. The Hangman will be in charge once the prisoners are in place. A drumroll will begin once the blindfolds are secure."

"Yes, sir, Colonel sir!" Mae and Luke began their awkward, shackled gait out the door of the brig and walked gingerly as they approached the platform, then up the nineteen steps. Once the

Hangman placed the hemp ropes around Mae and Luke's necks, he asked if either one had any final words. Luke shook his head in silence. Mae uttered at the top of her voice, "Death to Jomini!" The small crowd of military spectators, Secretary of War Feddelson among them, was struck by the statement. He alone chuckled slightly at hearing Mae's last words. The blindfolds were placed around their heads. The nooses were adjusted, chokingly taut around their necks. The drumroll commenced. A large lever was pulled, releasing the counterweights while simultaneously springing the trap doors, and the prisoners dropped approximately twenty feet to their deaths.

The drumroll ended, and the small crowd dispersed in silence shortly after the conclusion of the execution. The post-physician pronounced both prisoners dead of asphyxiation combined with severe neck trauma. Moments later, the front gates were opened, and reporters from all over swarmed in to officially report the results of the multiple hangings.

Mark and I stayed with the bodies of our slain family members as they were placed in wooden coffins and thrust on the back of a buckboard. The coffins were taken to an isolated corner of the post and buried with all the capital punishment victims whose sentences had been carried out prior to today. Two small, twelve-inch cubed blocks of granite with the roman numerals XXVII and XXVIII were put at the heads of the graves.

The End

www.ingramcontent.com/pod-product-compliance
Lightning Source LLC
Chambersburg PA
CBHW050001040726
47599CB00014B/1157